I0712985

COSCOM
ENTERTAINMENT

ALSO BY A.P. FUCHS


**BLOOD OF MY WORLD TRILOGY**

DISCOVERY OF DEATH
MEMORIES OF DEATH
LIFE OF DEATH


**UNDEAD WORLD TRILOGY**

BLOOD OF THE DEAD
POSSESSION OF THE DEAD
REDEMPTION OF THE DEAD


**THE AXIOM-MAN™ SAGA**
(LISTED IN READING ORDER)

AXIOM-MAN
EPISODE NO. 0: FIRST NIGHT OUT
DOORWAY OF DARKNESS
EPISODE NO. 1: THE DEAD LAND
CITY OF RUIN
EPISODE NO. 2: UNDERGROUND CRUSADE
OUTLAW
OF MAGIC AND MEN (COMIC BOOK)


**OTHER FICTION**

A STRANGER DEAD
A RED DARK NIGHT
APRIL (WRITING AS PETER FOX)
MAGIC MAN (DELUXE CHAPBOOK)
THE WAY OF THE FOG (THE ARK OF LIGHT VOL. 1)
DEVIL'S PLAYGROUND (WRITTEN WITH KEITH GOUVEIA)
ON HELL'S WINGS (WRITTEN WITH KEITH GOUVEIA)
ZOMBIE FIGHT NIGHT: BATTLES OF THE DEAD

Magic Man Plus 15 Tales of Terror
Undeniable

## Anthologies (as editor)

Dead Science
Elements of the Fantastic
Vicious Verses and Reanimated Rhymes: Zany Zombie
Poetry for the Undead Head
Metahumans vs the Undead
Bigfoot Terror Tales Vol. 1 (with Eric S. Brown)
Bigfoot Terror Tales Vol. 2 (with Eric S. Brown)
Metahumans vs Werewolves

## Non-fiction

Book Marketing for the
Financially-challenged Author
Canadian Scribbler: Collected Letters of an
Underground Writer
Look, Up on the Screen! The Big Book of
Superhero Movie Reviews
Getting Down and Digital: How to Self-publish
Your Book

## Poetry

The Hand I've Been Dealt
Haunted Melodies and Other Dark Poems
Still About A Girl

## Go to

**WWW.CANISTERX.COM**
**&**
**WWW.AXIOM-MAN.COM**

by

# A.P. FUCHS

COSCOM ENTERTAINMENT
WINNIPEG

The fiction in this book is just that: fiction. Names, characters, places and events either are products of the author's imagination or are used fictitiously. Any resemblance to actual events or persons living or dead, or any known superheroes and/or supervillains is purely coincidental.

ISBN 978-1-927339-51-0

Axiom-man and all other related characters are Trademark ™ and Copyright © 2013 by Adam P. Fuchs. All rights reserved.

AXIOM-MAN: OUTLAW is Copyright © 2013 by Adam P. Fuchs. All rights reserved, including the right to reproduce in whole or in part in any form or medium.

Published by COSCOM ENTERTAINMENT
www.coscomentertainment.com

Check out AXIOM-MAN on the web at
www.axiom-man.com

Text set in Garamond; Printed and Bound in the USA

COVER ART BY JUSTIN SHAUF AND KYLE ZAJAC

This is for my son Gabriel, whose namesake gave
Axiom-man his when the Saga began.

I love you, son.

# Axiom-Man™
# Outlaw

# PROLOGUE

"I HATE GIRLS who lie!" Corey screamed, slamming his fist right beside the young woman's head into the dumpster behind her. Had he not pulled the punch at the last second and lessened the impact, the blow would've broken his hand. Regardless, she deserved to be scared.

Tears ran down her cheeks, and not because of his sudden outburst. Corey had been watching Haley all night, right from when she stood on the corner off Higgins to when the john picked her up in a brown Chevy, to when they turned the corner and found a spot in an alley with burnt-out street lamps, straight through to when the john pulled out of the alley and dropped Haley off back near her post.

It was Haley's first night, a young girl of eighteen, needing some bucks to support her one-year-old at home. Her story was the classic tale of falling in love in high school, him being something of a jerk and treating her poorly, all the way to knocking her up then getting out of the relationship once the baby was born. Oh sure, he said he'd stick around forever—while she was pregnant—even made her believe him, but he was quickly proven false the day her contractions came hard and fast and it was time to go to the delivery room. He dropped her off at the hospital so she could check in and he'd go park the car.

To this day, he was still looking for a space.

And Corey didn't care. What he did care about was Haley was lying and saying she hadn't had any business all night, that she just stood there in the warm breeze, feeling like an idiot and had a change of heart about her taking part in the world's oldest profession.

But her tears betrayed her. Corey knew those tears. He'd seen them on a hundred girls. They were the tears of the shock of their first time, the ones that sprang up no matter how hard they tried to keep them down, the ones fueled by the knot in their stomach, the regret in their heart and the disbelief that good girls like themselves could sink so low and always—always— asking the question, "How did my life end up like this?"

He punched the dumpster again, this time with his other hand, making sure he planted his knuckles close to her ear. "Why you doing this, huh? Why you lying to me?"

"I swear, no . . . no one came b-by."

"Yeah? Then why you stuttering?"

"It's c-cold."

"Shut up! It's hot, muggy and you're sweating." At least, he was. He always tended to overdress and wear an extra layer.

"Well, I'm cold, okay?" She probably was, with that low-cut top and mini skirt.

She had guts, he'd give her that. "Haley, I saw you."

Her eyes went wide and she stopped blinking.

"You had a slow night, sure, but you had the one guy. I saw the whole thing. Pay up."

Shaking, her eyes not leaving his, she reached into the little, sparkling red purse she had slung over her shoulder and pulled out a couple hundred-dollar bills.

Corey yanked them from her hand. "He was generous, hm?" He eyed the hundreds then shoved them in his pocket.

He could see the heartbreak in her eyes. "Do I get—"

"Shut up!" He threw her to the ground. "You'll get yours when I break these bills."

"I need it tonight. My kid . . . my kid has had nothing all day. Just water."

"Not my problem. I said I'll give it to ya when I got it."

She grabbed his pant leg and gave it a tug. "Please," she said, "I'll do anything."

He knew what she meant and trying to bribe a guy in his position with something he could get anytime was unacceptable. He slapped her hard across the cheek, sending her back down. The reverberation from his palm connecting square with her cheekbone stung.

"Don't you ever try that with me again!" he shouted.

She reached for his pant leg again, clearly desperate. His job was to make an example of anyone who wouldn't play by the rules. He kicked her in the chest, sending her backward.

When she hit the ground, she said, "P-please . . ."

"Please nothing!" As she rolled onto her knees to get back up, he stomped on her lower back, causing her body to flatten and legs to jerk. Her chin hit the ground with a crack.

Whimpering, she said, "I can't bre—"

He kicked her in the ribs. "I know." This was too much fun. He kicked her again and heard something snap. He pulled his foot back, about to deliver another blow when he heard footsteps on the cement further down the alley in front of him. He immediately did a one-eighty and started running, not getting a glimpse of who it was. A rush of air passed over him and he quickly slammed into a figure clad in blue head-to-toe, a cape blowing gently behind him in the soft breeze.

Corey fell onto his behind and looked up at him. The diagonal light blue material over a dark blue bodysuit was a familiar sight; the same design adorned the mask on the man's face. He wore light blue gloves and brandished a golden yellow triangular belt buckle that somehow shone even in the dim lighting. Axiom-man stared down at him.

"You . . . you saw?" The words escaped Corey's lips without thinking.

"Everything."

Corey swallowed the lump in his throat. He'd heard about this guy. Who hadn't? There was only one place he'd be heading to in a few moments: jail.

The man reached down and with powerful hands pulled Corey up and set him on his feet. He spun him around so he was facing Haley, who lay still further down the alley. He shoved him forward.

"Well, what are you waiting for?" Axiom-man asked.

Corey peered over his shoulder. "What?" He was shoved forward again. He nearly did a face-plant from the force and flailed his arms to keep his balance.

"You're not finished with her yet."

"Are you crazy, man? You really think I'm going over there? I know who you are."

"I don't think you do."

The man shoved him forward again. The force of the blow was so much it caused his shoulder blades to buckle and his head to snap back. A sharp pain ignited in his neck.

"Finish her," the man said.

"Wha—" He was pushed forward again and this time fell down on all fours. He glanced up at Haley's body.

"You want to make her pay for trying to screw you out of some cash? Now's your chance. Make it right."

"What are you trying to do, man? Get me on more charges?"

"Helping you do your job. Don't make me throw you over there."

Shaking, Corey glanced back at the man in the blue cape. Perhaps despite all his do-gooding, this guy'd finally had enough of this city and wanted a harsher approach. Maybe he was getting guys like himself to somehow help?

"Promise you won't take me in if I do," Corey said and braced for impact.

None came.

"Promise," Axiom-man said.

He didn't have a choice and there was no way he could outrun the guy. Shakily, he got to his feet. "Okay." He walked over to Haley.

The man in the light blue cape was right behind him. Corey saw Haley's head turn in the man's direction and a flush of relief washed over her face when she saw him.

"Oh, thank God," she said as the caped man approached her.

The man booted her in the jaw, knocking her out. To Corey he said, "Your turn."

---

The man in blue had stopped Corey short of beating Haley to death. She was barely breathing, with broken bones in her face, hands, chest and probably a couple of other places. She was out cold from the pain and blood loss.

The man had stood there the whole time, hands at his side, simply watching.

Corey was trembling by the time he was done. When he backed away, he asked, "What now?"

The man in blue strode past him and knelt down beside Haley's body. When Axiom-man clenched his fists, Corey thought he was going to finish her off. Instead, the man administered something to her. Haley's head jerked as she came to. Her face was swollen, but he could still see her glazed-over eyes. Must've been smelling salts. The man gently positioned her head so she was looking in Corey's direction.

"Why'd you wake her up?" Corey asked.

The man stood, and without a word came over to him and pressed one hand over Corey's mouth and nose, the other against the back of his head. The pressure was enormous and immediately all of his air was cut off. Screaming against the iron-like palm, Axiom-man turned Corey's neck—slowly—further and further past the point of natural extension. At first, Corey tried to run and kick and punch, but his blows struck nothing but air as the man side-stepped each one, his strikes quickly slowing to nothing the further his neck was pushed past its natural range, the pain in his neck and spine locking up his entire body. His legs buckled beneath him and gave way, the man still holding all two hundred pounds of him up as if holding a child. Fire birthed in Corey's lungs as the hot pressure and need for air took over his chest cavity. The caped man had him as such that the man's elbows kept his torso in place and kept it from turning with his strained neck muscles. Soon, the steady deep clicks of his vertebrae grinding against each other filled his ears, the muscles in his neck burning as they were slowly torn.

He didn't know if the man was looking at him or at Haley. Darkness rimmed his vision and he soon thought of his mother. She didn't know of the life he led. It'd break her heart to find out. It was only supposed to have been temporary: a few years working this gig to make a few decent bucks before moving onto something else. He was going to give his mother some of the money so she could finally retire.

Heat rushed through Corey's muscles and every bone in his body completely locked. Through a lens of foggy realization, he understood his head was nearly clean right around and facing the back of his body. How the guy did it, he didn't know, but it seemed a learned technique.

A final rush of pain spiked over and through him just as the man's hand left the back of his skull and moved to the top his head.

Corey felt each pop of his skull as the man's fingers punctured through the bone.

All . . . five . . . fingers . . .

. . . before it went dark.

# CHAPTER ONE

NEARLY EVERYONE ON the bus looked as though they didn't want to be there. Gabriel Garrison felt the same as he sat there in the aisle seat near the rear door. His shift started at six in the morning today, just as it had ever since reporting for work the day after that crazy thing with Katie, someone, it turned out, who was in the preparation phase of one day taking to the crime-ridden streets and helping him clean them up. Not that he wouldn't mind the assistance, but Katie didn't have any special abilities aside from being the greatest martial artist he'd ever seen.

Not that he'd seen many others than in the occasional kung fu flick and a few MMA fights.

Ever since starting the early shift, he'd had a hard time adjusting, especially since he'd be on patrol until one or two as Axiom-man, sometimes longer depending on what went down. His boss, Rod Hunter, had cut him one last break on the attendance front. Before, Gabriel had his work performance to fall back on and was able to get some slack for either being late for work or not showing up at all—thanks to his duties as Axiom-man—but even that wore thin after a while. There was no grace left. One more absence, even if legitimate like him being sick, and he'd be out on his can. So said Rod, anyway. Gabriel wasn't sure if the guy would carry it out because the man had fired him once before then got him back onboard soon after, so it was hard to tell.

Either way, Gabriel knew his future wasn't at Dolla-card.

The problem, it would seem, was he wasn't cut out for much else and had no education other than high school.

He adjusted his glasses and ran his fingers through his brown hair, which he kept parted on the side. It was getting warmer out and between wearing his Axiom-man suit underneath his clothes plus shirt, tie and cardigan, he was having a hard time getting comfortable. Being on a cramped bus with barely any standing room didn't help either.

No matter. His stop was coming up in a few minutes anyway.

A couple of roughnecks toward the back, who were clearly high from sniffing something, were yapping overly loud and dropping the F-sharps pretty hard. A few seats down from them, a mother with her two little kids—probably two or three years old each, a boy and a girl with matching curly brown hair—held them tight to her body, covering their ears.

*Daycare run,* Gabriel thought. *Those guys should know better.* He thought again. *Yeah, right.*

One of the guys cussed out a few choice words in a row and was loud enough to make even the other people around him look at him.

"Excuse me," the mother said, "would you mind not swearing in front of my kids?"

The guy gave her a disgusted look, as if *she* was the one who'd done something wrong. "Why don't you shove it in your—" A fire truck with sirens blaring sped past the window, drowning him out.

Gabriel's gaze followed the fire truck through the window and he thought about getting off the bus, changing into his gear, then flying after it to see if his assistance was needed, but the commotion on the bus kept his attention here.

"How can you talk to people like that?" the mother asked.

The guy got out of his seat and stood over her.

Gabriel caught the bus driver glancing up at the ruckus in his rear-view mirror.

*Come on, man, do something,* he thought.

"Hey, cut it out," the bus driver said firmly.

"Yeah?" the guy said. "Do something."

Gabriel glanced at the mother tightly holding her kids against her. He could tell by the look in her eyes she was worried she had gone too far by speaking up. Her eyes met his. Gabriel shied away, but not because he wanted to.

Appearances.

Gabriel Garrison didn't get involved with street thugs. Only Axiom-man did.

Gabriel checked the bus driver's rear-view mirror again. The bus driver had his eyes back on the road. He knew from the chatter amongst cops that bus drivers weren't supposed to forcefully interfere but simply radio it in if things escalated.

The man stood over the woman, even went so far as pressing his legs right up against hers.

"Please, just go . . ." she said softly. The kids against her sides looked up at the man with worried eyes.

*Those two other big guys a seat over are watching the whole thing,* Gabriel thought. *So are you.* The whole secret identity argument didn't seem very valid right now especially after meeting Katie. She had kept herself—her *true* self—a secret until needed, then she showed what she was capable of. Gabriel knew he couldn't reveal his powers by *shifting* them on. His hair would turn blue and his eyes would glaze over in blue light. Everyone would know, and though the transformation would be enough to conceal his identity—he wouldn't need the mask—the happenings on city buses were recorded and it would only take a quick review of the tape to show which of the city's ordinary citizens was Axiom-man. His picture—even the transformation itself—would make the news and someone who recognized him would make a fuss by the afternoon.

The man looked over at his friend and they chuckled at each other.

The bus came to a stop at a red light. The bus driver got out of his seat and squeezed his way past the people and went to the back of the bus.

Gabriel saw the man take a deep breath for speaking. He was clearly nervous, and looked extremely out of shape with sweat-beading his brow beneath a head of gray hair.

"Back off," the bus driver said.

The man turned to him, grimaced, then gave him a shove. "Yeah?" He shoved him again. The bus driver stumbled back. "Why don't you go back to your seat and drive this thing like you're supposed to?" He shoved him one more time.

The driver fell by Gabriel's feet.

Gabriel stood, reached down and asked, "Are you okay?" He held out his hand.

The bus driver took it and Gabriel helped him up.

Everyone else on the bus just watched.

*Apathy. I hate it.*

"What about you, geek?" the man said, stepping right up to Gabriel. "Want me to throw you out? Door's right there."

Gabriel eyed him intently, knowing he could pull this guy apart if given the chance.

If his powers were activated, that was.

Without them he was an average guy with a couple of fists, but he'd been in enough fights going up against foes as equally-as-powerful or more so than him, so he had some experience under his belt duking it out. The guy in front of him probably had a lot of fighting experience, too, no doubt, given the scars around the guy's eyes.

"No thanks," was all Gabriel said. He had meant to cower and sit back down, but why were his feet planted? Had Katie rubbed off on him that much?

The man stepped onto the tops of Gabriel's dress shoes and put his nose against his.

"Leave him alone," the bus driver said and reached toward the man.

The man took a swing; his fist connected with the driver's jaw and knocked him down.

Gabriel took the opportunity and hooked the guy across the side of the head. The man spun and stumbled down the couple of steps leading to the back door. The door was closed, though, so the man lay there in a heap, scrambling to get his feet under him in the small space. Just then his buddy jumped in and took a swing at Gabriel. It looked like it was going to come in from the side so Gabriel went to move away, but instead the man changed tactics and delivered a swift uppercut to Gabriel's chin. His teeth slammed together, narrowly missing his tongue. Head rocking back, he felt a small pop at the back of his neck. His head spun and his neck hurt as he righted himself. Gabriel kicked out, catching the guy in the gut.

His friend was back up and about to tackle him to the ground.

Somehow the bus driver had gotten to the front of the bus and was hurrying everyone out.

With some room behind him now, Gabriel thought the "secret identity" thing to do would be to run away, but he'd been thinking about chucking the disguise anyway, at least the nerdy persona, as it had done him far more harm than good ever since adopting it.

The man shot in, grabbing Gabriel around the middle. Gabriel stumbled back, but with the guy tied up around his waist, he was able to bring his elbows down onto the man's back, catching him on either side of his spine. The man stopped his advance but still held on. Gabriel delivered the blow again and the guy backed away, reaching behind himself, wincing.

*Did some damage. Good.*

His friend came forward and started swinging. Gabriel ducked the first two shots, but caught the third square in the mouth. Lip inflating right away, he lowered his stance and punched the guy in the chest then in the stomach.

Sirens rose up somewhere outside the bus. Their sound didn't seem to faze the two punks trying to hurt him.

Gabriel kept edging toward the door. With the narrow aisle, room was limited so at least the guys couldn't charge him head-on.

He thought they wouldn't, anyway, but the two took a single file run toward him. Gabriel let the first guy come in close then put his elbow in the man's face, dropping him.

His friend shuffled around his fallen comrade and took a swing. Gabriel moved out of the way. The guy came in from the other side and hit Gabriel in the ear.

His glasses flew off, one of its arms scraping across his cheek as it did.

Gabriel stepped in, reached, and took the guy's head and slammed it into one of the grab poles next to a seat. The man's head bounced off it and he paused, dazed. Gabriel took his shot and punched the guy in the temple. The man fell.

It was over.

Ears ringing, Gabriel searched the floor and the seats for his glasses. He found them a couple spots down beneath one of the seats. He picked them up and wiped them on his shirt. He put them on and faced the front of the bus only to come face-to-face with a police officer.

"Care to tell me what just happened?" the cop asked.

"I'll tell them," the bus driver said, shame on his face. Looking Gabriel in the eye, he said, "Thank you."

------

It was already mid-morning by the time Gabriel finished up at the police station telling his side of the story. The recording from the bus's security cam showed what happened and how he'd come to the driver's aid. The bus driver let the cops have it and went on and on about policies of non-interference and how stupid they were.

He'd said more than a few times, "You guys better be thankful there are kids like this young man out there."

Gabriel'd been able to clean himself up at the downtown station, but his swollen lip and sore neck betrayed any concealment of his injuries never mind the dark red scrape along his cheek from when his glasses had been knocked off. He hadn't called into work and knew what was waiting for him when he showed up.

When he was leaving the building, he saw the mother in the foyer along with her children.

She came up to him. "Thank you."

"You're welcome. I'm glad they didn't hurt you, and thank you for standing by me in there." He nodded toward the back of the police station.

"Can't believe everyone just stood there."

He wanted to say, "Did you really expect anything else?" but didn't. It was a hard truth about people and their reaction to crime. Most, when seeing one taking place, simply looked on and waited for someone else to take action. Many also simply walked away. Gabriel knew that because long before the visit from the messenger and receiving his powers, he'd done the same thing on more than one occasion. Part of it was not knowing *how* to react and whether getting involved or not was the right thing to do. Another was the fear of getting beat up for doing so and putting his own interests and self-preservation above those of others.

"Hope you and your kids have a good day," Gabriel said.

"We will now," she said. "You're in our prayers, starting tonight."

"Thanks," he said. "Might need them."

As he walked to the office, he replayed the events on the bus over and over again in his mind. As good as it felt to stand up to those guys, it felt even better to do it out of costume. At the same time, to have the freedom to be helpful outside of the suit was something he wasn't used to. Whether out of habit or genuine feeling, a part of him regretted taking action in the context of blurring the lines between Gabriel and Axiom-man. He suddenly felt like the whole city knew who he really was.

*Just couldn't let them keep bugging that lady,* he thought.

His heart rate sped up the closer he got to Dolla-card. The plan would be to walk in, get things started at his desk, then wait for the inevitable call from Rod to come into his office. With each step forward, the lump in his throat grew bigger.

———

Gabriel had been at his desk for all of two minutes when Rod came up to his cubicle.

He must've caught sight of Gabriel's swollen lip or the scrape on his cheek because he said, "What happened?"

"Um . . . got mugged on the way here."

Rod ran his hands through his black hair, took a deep breath through his nose, and for a second Gabriel thought his boss had bought it. It wasn't an all-out lie as two guys *had* jumped him.

"Forget logging in," Rod said. "Grab your stuff and come with me."

Gabriel didn't have anything to bring other than himself so he shut down the computer and followed Rod to his office. Rod rounded to the other side of his desk and went for a small stack of papers already waiting. He picked them up, thumbed through them, then handed them to Gabriel.

The headline at the top of the first page made everything clear: GUIDELINES OF DISMISSAL.

Rod remained standing, but didn't make eye contact. "I'm sorry, Gabriel. Policy is policy and I've given you more chances than I've given anyone who's worked under me. There comes a time when even I have to answer to the higher-ups about these things."

"Can't you tell them I got mugged?" Gabriel asked. The words came out before he could think them through. Could've been the discomfort in his neck from eating that uppercut as the pain radiated from the ledge of his skull; his head was also still a little spinny. But the truth was, it was a deliberate play on a lie to save his own skin. He hated the lying part of being Axiom-man and did everything in his power when possible not to do it. Now his own butt was on the line and he didn't have a B-Plan for employment.

"No. You should've been here hours ago even if something did happen on the way to work. Did you call the police?"

If he said yes, Rod might follow up. How much info the police would disclose, Gabriel didn't know. All he said was, "I didn't call them." Which was true.

"Then why were you so late?"

"Recovery."

"Look, it won't matter. We had a guy who was repeatedly sick because of an autoimmune disease and the higher-ups didn't bat an eye. They stick to company guidelines like it's the Bible. I'm really sorry, Gabriel. I can't cover for you anymore otherwise it's my can on the line and I can't lose my job."

"But I can?"

Rod's eyes finally met his.

"I don't have anything else and I can barely afford to live on what I make here."

Rod's brow furrowed.

"What I mean is, I don't have much savings and going on unemployment won't cover my day-to-day though I live cheap. Cheap-cheap."

Rod sighed and seemed to consider his words.

Gabriel couldn't believe his own tone of panic coming out of his mouth. Tangle with a supervillain? Sure. Go up against two sniffed-out punks on the bus? No problem. But lose his job with nothing to fall back on? He'd pick the former any day. What would happen to Axiom-man if he didn't have a place to hang his cape?

"Gabriel," Rod said, his voice soft, "I'm sorry. I really am, but I'm going to have to let you go."

Gabriel's heart sunk. So this was it.

"I'll give you a reference for whatever it is you do next, okay?"

He nodded. As if that made it better.

Rod looked at the papers in Gabriel's hand. "I need you to fill those out, just exit interview stuff." Gently, he added, "You were a good employee. Seriously. One of the best. There was never an issue come review time and you always went above and beyond for the customer." He paused. "When you were here. Dolla-card appreciates that."

*Sure, rub it in.* "Glad to be of help, I guess. I'm sorry, Rod. I really am." He never called Rod by his first name and always kept the formality as part of his respectful nerdy persona. Today it didn't matter and Rod didn't seem to notice.

"Me, too. You can fill those out here. I'll also talk to HR and make sure you get two weeks' severance, any vacation pay owing, and any upsell commissions you had on your tracking sheet."

"Want me to get it for you?"

"I'll get it. You can't go back to your desk. I'm required to have security escort you out when you're done."

Even after all this time, after all the hard work he'd done for the company, he'd still go out like some Joe who'd only been there a couple weeks and blew it.

"I'm sorry again, Gabriel."

"Me, too."

He finished up the papers and a security guard came and got him. As he left Rod's office, all eyes were on him and he could only imagine what was going through their heads:

*Did he steal something?*

*Gabriel? Canned?*

*Whatever.*

*Hope my job is safe.*

*Never liked that guy anyway.*

As he rode down the elevator, Gabriel thought about his time at Dolla-card. It really was an end of an era. Even that modification he'd made to the door leading to the roof so he could quickly change and leave the building as Axiom-man seemed like something he did somewhere else far away in another life.

The security guard escorted him out the doors without a word. Even when Gabriel gave him a thank you as a courtesy, the man said nothing, and went back into the building.

Neck aching, Gabriel looked up and down the street, feeling lost. It was one thing to have a day off and roam around downtown; quite another knowing he was supposed to be at work with the security and routine of that having been taken away.

He shoved his hands in his pockets and licked his swollen lip. When he got home, he'd put some ice on it. The back of his head and neck ached. That guy had really cranked him.

He might have to see a chiropractor, and he didn't even have coverage. Not anymore.

# CHAPTER TWO

Patrons sat in the King's Head Pub, enjoying a beer with a late lunch. The room was alive with chatter.

From behind the bar, Pete poured another customer a drink. "That's five-fif—" A loud crash shook the room as a car came flying through the window on his left, taking out those sitting closest to it, tearing them to the floor. The car tumbled past the bar, taking out the lights overhead, the tables, chairs, and slammed into the pool tables beyond, blasting them into splinters and knocking down the handful of patrons around them.

Pete stood there, leg-locked, heart racing, mouth hanging open. Those in the side area of the pub came rushing to see what happened. Screams filled the place as well as groans of pain and the wails of panic.

Legs like rubber, Pete shuffled his way to the smashed window, side-stepping bits of the surrounding wall and heaps of glass that came crashing in with the vehicle. At the edge of the window, looking down a half storey to the street, Pete's breath caught in his throat.

Axiom-man stood in the middle of the road across from the place, staring right at him.

---

Gabriel sat on the sofa in his apartment, shirt off, pants on, his costume revealed underneath. Pressing an ice cube wrapped in a paper towel to his lip, he went over the morning's events for the tenth time.

"Can't believe I got fired," he muttered. He knew it wasn't his fault; he never deliberately chose to be absent for selfish reasons. Still, it sucked, and he was being penalized—when it came right down to it—for doing the right thing.

He ran the numbers through his head and breathed a sigh of relief to know—with his upcoming severance pay, the vacation pay and commissions, plus his meager savings—he'd be okay for at least the next six weeks, which pretty much meant he'd have to go on the job hunt no later than tomorrow as—from what he'd overheard at work from others who had friends looking for employment—response time from employers was slow these days with little job availability out there. One person, he'd heard, had taken three months to find something once they started looking.

"I don't have three months," Gabriel said and slurped down some of the water melting off the ice.

*I could ask my parents for a loan, maybe. They can't cover much, but it could be enough to see me through an extra month or two if I eat nothing but Ramen noodles.* One thing was certain: he didn't want to move back home. To try and be Axiom-man while living under his parents' roof would be near impossible. He needed the freedom of being out on his own and the ability to get up and go at all hours for any reason. There was no way that would fly at home without them questioning what he was doing leaving the house at two in the morning if something came up, regardless of how old he was. Never mind if he came home battered and bruised like today. The probing would be endless.

He thought maybe he could get in touch with Valerie Vaughan, ask her to maybe pull a string or two—if she had any to pull, that was—and get him a job working at Owen Tower. It's where she had gone after Dolla-card. Maybe there was something there? But he hadn't talked to

Valerie in a long time, not since she'd been kidnapped and he rescued her, only later in the hospital room to have her tell him to leave her alone.

Gabriel knew he had scared her. When he had come crashing through that basement ceiling and began dishing it out to her captors, he let go and nearly killed the guy, bashing his head to a pulp. So far as he knew, the guy was permanently damaged and needed years of reconstructive surgery to look halfway decent again.

What made that hospital visit painful wasn't that she had gotten mad at Axiom-man. It was that she had revealed she knew who he really was. How she figured it out, he didn't know as he had been so careful to keep Gabriel and Axiom-man as two separate people. Somehow, Valerie had recognized him beneath the costume.

There was so much he wanted to tell her, so much he wanted to reveal to her, and give her a chance to know the guy—the *real* guy—beneath the suit. She only knew Gabriel as a nice-guy-wimpy-loser and Axiom-man as the brave hero. She never knew the Gabriel he was when he wasn't wearing the cape or the glasses.

Not the one who sat on his sofa worried he'd be homeless in a half-dozen weeks.

Not the one who sat there thinking about her, worrying about her, needing her comforting presence.

Not the one who so desperately wanted to reach for the phone and beg her to meet with him whether in costume or out.

———

Herb hated his new job. The pizza part of it was a perk as the place he worked for gave employee's fifty percent off whether on shift or off, but delivering the pizzas—that he hated. He had to use his own car, and the pizza joint only reimbursed the gas not any wear and tear, or the cost of any repairs that might need to be conducted if something happened while on the road. Like two months ago when he ran over a nail in a back lane and, when a couple patch jobs didn't hold, had to buy a new tire. He'd been a higher-up administrator for the City prior to this, but with cutbacks and a few interoffice politics that didn't sit well with those who didn't like him, well, he was out on his can and this pizza delivery gig was the only thing he could find for the time being.

He drove into the North End, eyes peeled, knowing the area's reputation for being one a person shouldn't walk around alone in at night. Even during the day, for that matter. Not that it was terribly late right now. It was close to six and he was doing a pizza supper run.

When he approached the house, he pulled up tight to the curb, set the car in park, then grabbed the insulated bag of pizza off the seat. The place was rundown and he had to walk up close to the house to verify the tiny iron numbers close to the door.

He rang the bell. A moment later, a big burly dude with a shaved head and moustache opened the door.

"Pizza," Herb said.

The man glanced up from the insulated bag; his eyes met Herb's then quickly shifted to something beyond.

Furrowing his brow, Herb said, "What?" and turned around.

Axiom-man stood behind him.

*Hope this guy isn't in trouble,* Herb thought. *What kind of house did they send me to?*

In one smooth motion, blue-gloved fists grabbed him by the collar and Axiom-man brought Herb's head crashing into his. Stars burst before Herb's vision as he was thrown to the ground. The man in the blue cape stepped up to the big guy at the door, who quickly took a swing at the costumed crusader. Axiom-man ducked and put his fist *through* the man's head. When he yanked it out, blood and brain came with it.

Axiom-man came over to Herb, kicked him in the ribs; they snapped from the blow. He stomped on Herb's arm, cracking the bone like a dry twig. Axiom-man stepped into the house and as Herb laid there dazed, he heard the screams of children rise in pitch and volume until what sounded like the slamming of bodies against walls silenced them.

---

The swelling in his lip pretty much receded, Gabriel booted up the computer, sat down in front of it, and got to work eating last night's leftover pizza while the system loaded. He was going to save searching the want ads for tomorrow, but figured he might as well get a head start and give them a browse before heading out on patrol.

Having not eaten since that morning, he made quick work of the first leftover slice. The second and final one he made a conscious decision to try and savor.

"Might need to get used to eating less . . . stretch the buck," he said with a mouth full of cheese.

Once the system loaded, he pulled up a Web browser and Googled the local job bank. When his search loaded, he clicked on the link. Right after, another window popped up in the corner of the screen. It was an email alert service that kept him posted on news stories that contained certain keywords, ones he adjusted now and then depending on his needs, what was going on in the city, and anything he might've overheard while listening in on conversations in the bars under his guise as "Mike," a rough-around-the-edges persona he created in an effort to get closer to the city's underground. It was under that guise he met Katie and learned of the Russian mob's influence in the city, dirty cops, and something called the Enhancer, a wonder formula that transformed ordinary people into super athletic ones.

"Axiom-man" was one of the keywords since at first it had been a bit of ego-stroking and he wanted to see what others were saying about him in the media, but then he changed his attitude and made it about encouragement, seeing firsthand how much of a positive impact Axiom-man was having on society and the world, and if folks were following his example of trying to make the planet a better place.

The story that came up, however, made him read the headline twice: AXIOM-MAN ON A RAMPAGE?

The article was brief, but mentioned Axiom-man allegedly to have been connected with the murder of a pimp's errand boy last night along with being responsible for throwing a car through a window at the King's Head this afternoon. The survivor of last night's incident saw what Axiom-man did and was being held up in a hospital, but the article didn't say which one.

Someone masquerading as Axiom-man and causing trouble to give him a bad rep was a possibility Gabriel had kept in the back of his mind for quite some time, but this person going so far as murder? Not to mention having the strength to throw a car through a window?

Redsaw?

*But he hasn't been around since the night the Doorway opened. Why would he surface now?* He knew Redsaw would show up again at one point. He was destined to fight the man, probably to the death, at one point in the future. But nothing in this article indicated a display of flight or red energy beams emitted from "Axiom-man's" hands.

"Jack's going to have a field day with this," he said.

Jack Gunn, captain of the Special Force Unit, had an edgy relationship with Axiom-man at best, and after what happened at Tireland and Katie revealing Jack's dark side, suggesting he answered to higher-ups who didn't have the city's best interest at heart—Jack was going to be bad news and soon.

Was that who this Axiom-man imposter was? Had the Enhancer gotten out? Katie said it didn't bestow super-powered abilities on a person, just amped them up past Olympic-level athleticism. Unless ultra strength happened to be what she meant by "past." She also hinted at it causing a genetic mutation, but didn't have any information as to what that mutation was.

Gabriel re-read the article then did a search for the same headline. Only a couple repeats of the same story came up. He scanned his email alert service for any other local stories talking about death, destruction of property, Axiom-man, and found none.

Winnipeg's news services weren't always on the cutting edge nor were things reported up-to-the-minute, so the delay was understandable. This also meant something else could be happening out there right now and he wouldn't know about it until possibly as late as tomorrow.

No time for resting on his laurels eating. It was time to hit the skies, and he only had one lead: the girl at the hospital.

# CHAPTER THREE

IF THE GIRL was anywhere, it was most likely at the Health Sciences Centre located downtown. It was the closest hospital to the incident last night.

Axiom-man kept himself high above the hospital building, using the night sky as part of his cover to keep himself from any eyes looking up. He circled the building and saw a few cop cars parked out front, one in the back. Their presence might or might not be related, but there was a good chance one of them belonged to an officer guarding the room, if there was one. That would be his tell. To fly around the building and look in each of the windows wouldn't reveal anything as there would be multiple female patients, and unless a cop was right inside the room with her, there would be nothing to set her apart from the rest. The cop would have to be outside the room by the door or close to it.

*Wait . . . she'd probably be in the ER, maybe even the ICU.* There was no seclusion there as he'd been to the ER a couple of times himself, both before and after becoming Axiom-man. Getting in could be an issue.

"This sucks," he said. *I need to know what she saw.* "Unless . . ." He couldn't go to the pub as anyone who had been there when the car came through the window would be gone and the place would be taped up. There was no way to track down who had been there anyway in any reasonable amount of time.

The girl was his only option.

Keeping his distance from the hospital, Axiom-man flew to an alleyway and landed. Once he touched down, he dug in the thin backpack he kept beneath his cape and pulled out some civilian clothes: plaid shirt, jeans, loafers and a baseball hat. No glasses. It was time for "Mike" to see what he could find out, and with the scrape across his cheek from earlier, it only added to his rough-and-tumble appearance should someone get a good look at him.

A few minutes later, he emerged from the alleyway and, keeping his head down to avoid people looking at his face but without suspiciously doing so, he made his way across the street and headed for the ER entrance.

Once inside, he surveyed the waiting room. It was packed as usual. He took a quick note of the cameras, careful not to give them a full view of his face. With another glance of the room, he feigned a coughing fit and made his way over to the surgical masks that were out for those wishing to use them in the interest of germ protection. Once the mask was on, he faked relief from what came over him and, since the room was busy and there was a line up at reception, he had no trouble blending in as someone who'd already been registered.

A few minutes later, he found the double doors leading into the ER proper where doctors saw patients. With visiting hours nearly over, he had to make this quick so he did a swift walk-through and found a room in the middle of a hallway off to the side, a cop sitting outside the door on a chair.

If the WPD were anything, they were predictable and stationing a cop in plain view outside of someone of interest's hospital room seemed protocol 101.

*Just got to draw him away.* Gabriel thought back to Katie and how she had been able to get her friend Ben out of a crowded police station by setting off the fire extinguishers and clouding the air. Obviously doing something like that here would be completely out of the question. There was no way he could draw the cop away from his station without causing a major ruckus, which could in turn affect patients who seriously needed care, and he didn't want to be responsible for someone dying and-or not being attended to because of his actions.

Was someone in the room with the girl?

He couldn't linger in the hallway long lest he bring suspicion on himself. He feigned another coughing fit just to keep up appearances, but was careful enough not to draw every eye in the ICU on him.

This wasn't the movies so he couldn't go find a pair of scrubs and pretend to be a doctor or a nurse. The safest bet would be to take note of the room's positioning and locate it from the outside and come in through the window. Learning from Katie that being well-versed in one's surroundings was paramount to the success of a mission, he kept his head down and walked past the room with the cop stationed outside of it. Glancing in through the small window in the door, he saw the room had no windows so wouldn't be accessible from the outside.

*Now I'm screwed*, he thought.

Gabriel walked to the end of the hallway and saw the bathroom on the left. He went in and glanced up.

*My only option*, he thought. He flicked the light on and locked the bathroom door and *shifted* on his powers. Rising off the ground, he floated to the ceiling and examined the tile. It was the kind that was dry-walled in place. Knowing he didn't have a choice, he cut out one of the tiles with his eye beams and proceeded upward to the T-bar system that held the tiling in place, and maneuvered his way through the dark, using the faint glow of his eyes as a guide until he thought he was over the girl's room. He pierced a small hole through the tile from the opposite side.

*Wrong room,* he thought, seeing an old man lying in a bed, his wrinkled mouth wide open as he slept. He tried again about ten feet over to the right. *There.* He could see the door and the top of the cop's head through the small window in it. Hooking his finger in the hole, he held the tile in place as he cut out a space big enough for him to squeeze through, then went down into the room.

The young woman lay there in the bed hooked up to a couple of I.V.s, her face in bandages, same with her arms. It looked like she was wearing a body cast, but it was hard to tell since the bed sheets covered most of her.

She was sleeping.

*She's going to scream when she sees me.* He *shifted* off his powers. Her waking to a pair of floating, glowing blue eyes in the dark was not what she needed right now.

He put a hand over her mouth and with the other shook her shoulder. "Hey," he whispered.

When she didn't stir, he gave her a good shake. Her eyes slowly opened and he had to press down on her mouth to muffle her scream.

"I'm not going to hurt you, I promise," he said. "It's me. It's Axiom-man."

Her muffled scream intensified and Gabriel shot a glance over at the door, half-expecting the cop to bust in on them.

"Quiet!" he whispered as loudly as he could. "I promise I won't hurt you. I need to talk to you because who you saw last night wasn't me."

She quivered beneath him and he felt like the biggest goon for being so rough with her.

"I'm going to remove my hand. If you scream, that cop outside is going to come in and maybe even shoot me, but if you don't tell me what you saw, I won't be able to stop who really did this to you." He tried to be as gentle as he could with his words, but also ensured they had an edge to them so she knew he was serious and wasn't fooling around. "I'm going to take my hand off at the count of three. What happens next is up to you. I'll even stand a few feet away and raise my hands so you know you're safe. Ready? One, two, three." He let go and backed off, raising his palms shoulder height, peaceably. He hoped she could at least see his silhouette from the faint light coming into the room from the window in the door.

She lay there breathing heavily through her nose. The poor woman was terrified and he couldn't blame her.

"What's your name?" he asked.

She hesitated for several long seconds before saying, "H-Haley."

"Nice to meet you, Haley. I want to help, but I need you to stay calm. Can you do that for me?"

"I'll-I'll try." Her fear-filled eyes never left him.

"Okay. I know you think I put you in here. I didn't. It wasn't me. It was someone dressed like me."

"I-I was beat up first. You—I mean, if what y-you say is t-true—that guy, the other . . . you . . . only kicked me once. Corey. His name was Corey. He beat me up real bad. Then you . . . that other Axiom-man showed up and got me. Then he turned my head and . . . I saw it. I saw him twist Corey's neck around so far he was like an owl. Then he . . . I-I can't say it."

"You have to. I need to know."

"He crushed his skull with his bare hands. It was like an egg in his fingers. He squeezed and that sound" —her voice rose in volume— "that sound!"

"Shhh." He glanced toward the door. No one came.

She was back to whispering again and spoke quickly, presumably from panic. "I'll never forget it. He crushed his skull and killed him. After, when he dropped the body, he looked at me as if to make sure I was still conscious, still watching. The police and EMTs showed up very soon after." She coughed. Gabriel checked the door. They were safe. "I was thinking about it. There was no way they would've randomly found me unless someone tipped them off and I don't think anyone else was watching. It's like that guy . . . wanted me to be found. There's no reason to have kept . . . to have kept me alive otherwise."

"Anything else? Could he do anything special? Did he fly?"

She tried shaking her head but stopped herself and winced. Gabriel could only imagine the kind of pain she was in. "The only thing was he had picked Corey off the ground and held him up there as if it was nothing. Never knew someone could be that strong." She paused. "Are *you* that strong?"

"Strong enough. Is there anything else, Haley?"

"I'm scared. I'm scared that he'll come after me and kill me."

"He won't." Gabriel couldn't guarantee that, but it was all he could say. The woman was clearly terrified. "I'm going to find him and stop him."

"You should tell the police."

"They won't believe me."

"Why?" she asked.

"It's a long, complicated story." He kept his hands up and took a step closer. When she tensed up on the bed, he stopped his advance. "Sorry. I just want to say thank you for your help. Please, don't let them know I was here. Please promise you'll keep that a secret."

"I'll-I'll try."

"I need you to promise."

"Why?"

"Because they might think I came here to hurt you or threaten you to keep you quiet. Maybe worse. I'm going to make this right, Haley. You have to trust me. Please try to trust me."

"O-okay."

"Okay." He *shifted* his powers on and he didn't need to see himself from her perspective to know she saw a pair of glowing blue eyes light up in the dark. Gabriel floated to the ceiling and replaced the tile as best he could without it falling through the hole he created. A crack around two sides of it was inevitable as it lay on top from the other side of the ceiling, but he hoped no one noticed.

Back in the rafters, he returned to the glowing yellow square in the distance, the light from the bathroom. Out of the crawlspace and inside the single-stall room, he affixed the ceiling tile as best he could akin to the one in Haley's room, floated to the floor then *shifted* his powers off.

He opened the bathroom door and emerged in the hallway. A staircase was at the end. It'd be easier than having to go back the way he came so he headed toward it. When he saw the bold red lettering on the door saying an alarm would sound if used, he sighed knowing he'd have to go all the way back through the ICU and through the ER to get outside.

Hopefully there wouldn't be an issue as he made his way through since visiting hours were over.

# Chapter Four

Around midnight, Captain Jack Gunn came out of 7-11, coffee in hand, none too pleased he'd been put on the late shift, but with reports of Axiom-man having gone rogue, and as head of the Special Force Unit, he was to be on call, no questions asked.

He got into his squad car, tried taking a sip of his coffee, then set it down in the holder after he burned his tongue. He needed the recharge and had little patience for waiting right now.

The squawk box came to life: *Attention all units near Lombard and Main. Explosion at Bailey's Restaurant and Bar. Fire and paramedics on the way. Special call one-one-three-eight. Repeat, special call one-one-three-eight.*

Code One-One-Three-Eight. That was meant for him specifically. Not everyone knew the code for Special Force Incident. This meant there was another situation with Axiom-man involved or on the scene.

Jack fired up the sirens and peeled out of the 7-11 parking lot. He eyed his cup of joe all the way there, wondering if it was getting cool enough for a sip.

---

For the past hour, Axiom-man combed the airways above the city, keeping an eye out for anything or anyone that might be up here that would indicate who was mimicking him. He saw nothing and thought maybe he was jumping the gun thinking it was another person with special abilities or even Redsaw. Or, worse, an evil version of himself that came through one of the portals the black clouds created. It'd happened before, an evil alternate version of himself. There was one in that world of the undead he had visited.

Haley could've been mistaken in what she saw, with the fake Axiom-man lifting that Corey guy off the ground like a Teddy bear. The poor girl was half out of it and her mind could've easily been playing tricks on her.

Axiom-man rubbed his neck. He was still sore from that uppercut on the bus earlier. If it didn't let up by morning, he'd have to see somebody, coverage or none. It'd be a hindrance to him serving the public if he was injured never mind if he had to throw down with whoever was terrorizing the city.

Coming up over the heart of downtown, he saw an orange glow rising off the streets in the distance.

*Fire,* he thought. He brought his fists together and kicked on the speed, hoping the blaze was minor.

---

Jack pulled up just down the street from Bailey's, which was fully ablaze and with flame spitting out the windows. The few trees lining the street out front were lit up like giant torches. He heard sirens on the air, which indicated the fire department and paramedics were nearby and should roll up soon.

He ran and got as close as he could, the heat from the inferno staggering even some twenty feet away.

People hanging around the surrounding bars started lining the street, looking on in shock and disbelief.

"Go on, get out of here!" he shouted at them, but they didn't budge, just looked at him as if he had no place to tell them anything. Figuring they didn't know he was a cop thanks to his trench coat and not a uniform, he flashed his badge. They still stood there. *Idiots.*

The heat coming off the place was ferocious. An explosion came from inside the building, causing Jack to jump back a step and send his heart racing.

He scanned the area, namely the rooftops.

He pulled his gun when he saw a caped figure atop the Grain Exchange Building next door.

---

Axiom-man flew over the fiery scene and recognized the building aflame as belonging to Bailey's. The whole front of the building was blown out and scattered across the street, some of the debris having smashed the cars parked out front, bits of them on fire. He feared that if they kept alight, the cars would overheat and eventually the gas tanks would get tapped and they'd explode.

More and more people began gathering a safe distance around, though the black smoke quickly filling the area was making it increasingly difficult to see. Way down the street he saw the flashing lights of the approaching fire trucks. They'd get things started as soon as they arrived, which was good, but in the meantime he had to ensure nobody got hurt.

He flew down lower and noticed Jack was there, gun drawn, looking at something on a rooftop across the way. Axiom-man followed his line of sight; there was a shadowy caped figure atop the Grain Exchange Building, looking down.

Furious, as this was clearly the perpetrator, Axiom-man flew toward the person standing there. Before he could get a good look, an explosion went off below as one of the cars out front blew up from the heat.

People gasped and screamed as shrapnel and debris flew off in all directions. Another car went off, this one going up in the air then tumbling down the street toward the civilians like a bowling ball gone rogue.

Axiom-man immediately flew toward it, his first instinct to try and catch it, but with the car's weight combined with the momentum, he knew he wasn't strong enough. Besides, he'd singe his hands the second he touched the hot metal. His only choice was to—

He activated his eye beams and cleaved the vehicle in two, the force from the blast enough to send each piece off in separate directions. One crashed into another car further down the street, triggering its alarm, the other losing speed as it jumped the curb and hit a series of enormous cement planters housing flowerbeds across the way.

He landed.

Fire trucks pulled up close to the building. Men jumped out and got right to work.

Amidst the roar of the flame, Axiom man made out two words from a familiar voice: "Don't move."

Axiom-man turned around.

"I said don't move, dirt bag." Jack had the gun aimed right at him. If he fired, Axiom-man would take one to the chest.

Axiom-man looked past Jack to the rooftop across the way. The caped figure was gone.

"Backup's going to be here any minute and I'm taking you in. Don't think I can't either. We got certain . . . upgrades . . . and I know for one thing you ain't bulletproof." Jack fished inside his trench coat and pulled out a Taser. "Probably ain't electric-proof either."

"You got an inferno here, Jack," Axiom-man shouted above the flames. "You think shooting me is going to fix it? Look, I know you think I did it, but I'm telling you the truth: I didn't."

"Guilty parties usually start out with the whole 'wasn't me' thing. Been there, done that. Try another one. I saw you up on that rooftop surveying your handiwork."

"Do you really think I'd stick around to bask in the glow of it if I did, never mind come down here to street level and stand in front of it?"

"Maybe. Depends if you're trying to set yourself up as the innocent one, just like you're doing now. 'It wasn't me, Jack. It was an imposter.' Shut up." More sirens filled the air. "There's my guys. Don't even think about escaping."

The rush of water gushing from the fire hose masked even the roar of the inferno.

"If you're going to take me in," Axiom-man shouted, "then at least take me in alive. Both of us are in danger if something else blows."

Jack seemed to consider his words. Readjusting his grip on the gun and reaffirming his footing, he said, "Slowly."

Axiom-man raised his hands and walked past Jack, leading them both away from the flames. The last thing he needed was for something to happen to Gunn and then be blamed for that as well.

Once clear of the fire, Jack said, "Down the street, toward the car." He nodded in the direction of a Special Force Unit vehicle pulling up.

*Some "car,"* Axiom-man thought. He glanced back at Bailey's and saw shadows on the roof. He pointed upward. "Jack, there're people up there!"

"I'm not falling for that. You want me to turn around and—"

An officer ran up to Jack then followed Axiom-man's pointing finger.

"Captain Gunn, there's people up on the roof."

Jack turned; Axiom-man took the opportunity and flew up toward the top of the building. Jack was many things, but unless he'd gone completely reckless, he wouldn't shoot him down, not with innocent lives at stake.

Axiom-man didn't bother looking back at Jack, not wanting the captain to take it as an I-told-you-so and only fan the flame.

On the roof was a handful of men in nice suits and a couple of ladies in gorgeous evening gowns. Bailey's was a pretty classy place and a great joint for some late-night drinks and atmosphere. At most, Axiom-man would be able to carry down four people at a time. It'd take two trips if he took them down to street level and he knew when he did, Jack would have a couple of guns on him the moment he touched down the second time.

There was a parkade across the way. It'd have to do.

Axiom-man landed on the roof. They looked relieved to see him. To the first of the men, a young guy, probably his own age, Axiom-man said, "I'm going to fly you guys across then you're on your own."

"Good. Okay. Whatever. Just get us out of here." The man's words were a little slurred, probably from having one too many.

"Ladies first." Axiom-man approached the two women, instructed them to come in close while he held one on either side around the waist, then told the man he'd just spoken to to grab on from the back and instructed another to hold on from the front. When they got on, he floated off the ground, but not too high to further accelerate their panic; just enough to get them clear of the roof and to the parkade across the way. He heard one of them gasp when they crossed several stories above the alleyway between the back of the restaurant and the parkade.

He landed. The men immediately released their holds, the other two were so scared he had to specifically tell them to let go.

Turning back, crazy amounts of steam had risen off the street as the firemen doused the flames, smoke and steam quickly billowing across the roof. Those remaining on top ran across to the rooftop's edge closest to the parkade to try and get out of harm's way.

"No!" Axiom-man shouted. *The heat'll kill 'em!* He gave it everything he had and flew from the parkade's roof back to the restaurant's. He didn't touch down and instead told them to grab on the way the previous group did. They all jumped on him like a bunch of football players going after the ball. Fighting their force to pull him down, he wrapped his legs around the two on either side, held one in front, the other in back, and flew straight up as quickly as he could as hot steam and smoke blanketed the rooftop.

The men screamed from the rush and he felt one of them slipping.

"Hold on!" he said and felt the guy readjust his grip. The guy kept clawing at him but wasn't getting any traction; it'd only be a matter of seconds before he'd fall.

With his hands tied up holding the men in front and back, he couldn't help him. He punched it and flew as high as he could. The guy let go and screamed, falling. Axiom-man kept up the speed. It'd take too long to drop off these three on the parkade then try and save the other guy so he flew the other three to the nearest rooftop, shaking them off and letting them fall the remaining ten feet before he swooped toward the man falling from the sky. He came up behind him and hooked his hands under the man's arms and slowed his decent just above street level.

The guy kept screaming even as Axiom-man returned him to his friends.

"You crazy?" one guy said as Axiom-man touched down. "You nearly broke my leg dropping me like that."

"You're alive."

The guy pointed a stern finger at him. "You're crazy."

"You're welcome."

Another guy piped up. "Don't listen to him. Thanks, man. We owe you one."

Axiom-man rose into the sky. "Don't mention it. Just calm your friends down."

"How're we supposed to get off here?"

"I'll let someone know you're up here. Just be patient. They'll come, or if you got a cellphone, 911 it."

The guy pulled out his phone. "I'll call. Hope they don't arrest me."

"Tell them about the fire and to talk to your friends on the parkade. It'll be all right."

"Thanks again," one of them said.

Axiom-man rose higher. "That's what I'm here for." And flew off.

# Chapter Five

OSCAR OWEN HAD been up all night. Now, around seven in the morning, he sat at the island in his kitchen, cup of coffee in hand, staring at the gray and black marble countertop.

An excited fire burned in his belly at the notion that his exile was almost over. Though the public had been made aware of Oscar's activities as CEO of Owen Enterprises, the completion of Owen Tower and its upcoming grand opening, Redsaw had been gone from the public eye for quite some time.

*Soon,* he thought. The desire to put on the red and black suit was returning and the thirst for the power it represented never left. After the night the Doorway opened, he needed to step back, reassess, and reflect on what he had become. Each death he caused made him more powerful and, eventually, enabled him to cut through the dimensional fabric of the universe and open the Doorway of Darkness. Inside it, he conversed with his master and learned of his destiny.

It would soon be time to bring it about, but first he needed to ensure Axiom-man would no longer be a threat.

The man in the blue cape had to die . . . but not just yet.

Oscar thought of the Redsaw suit he kept locked away in his den. He had to time his re-emergence right, catch Axiom-man off guard and end him, no holding back.

But first, he had to finalize the details for Owen Tower's grand opening ceremony next week. While the offices within were already in full swing, this formality with the public had yet to take place. Once the media got hold of the tower's official launch, his company could pursue plans to build a tower in every major city nationwide. Requests from businesses looking for more affordable leasing were already pouring in once word spread of the first tower's construction. Finding funding for the project wasn't an issue and already several hundred million dollars had been secured. To have a stronghold in each city, Oscar relished the thought because the towers represented something more than just simple buildings.

They were homing beacons.

———

Gabriel rolled out of bed around nine, sleeping in later than he intended. After the late night, his body wouldn't let him get out of bed when the alarm went off at eight. As he hobbled to the bathroom, he couldn't believe the stench of smoke on his skin even after shedding his costume. A shower was in order, then breakfast while checking the news.

When he was done getting himself together, he poured a bowl of cereal and booted up the computer. With this madman pretending to be Axiom-man on the loose, he'd check the headlines first then, depending on what they yielded, start up on the job market before making a trip to the unemployment office that afternoon. He hoped he'd get approved, especially since he got canned, and simply being out of work wasn't enough to reclaim that mandatory money a person had to put into E.I. every check. There were a few hoops you had to jump through first, never mind doing a song and dance while juggling bowling balls and balancing a piano on your head.

As he ate his cereal, Gabriel combed the headlines and the fifth one read: AXIOM-MAN MANHUNT UNDERWAY. He nearly choked. There had been another hit last night, this one at a house in the North End and . . .

"Children," he said quietly through a mouth full of cereal. The article went on to state that four kids were found beaten to death with broken bones inside a home, and the father had a hole punched through his face. The inside of the house was destroyed, the pizza delivery guy who had witnessed the man's death left alive to tell the tale, but not without having several of his ribs broken along with his arm.

*"I thought he protected us,"* the pizza guy had said in the article. *"Those kids. I heard them screaming and I couldn't help 'em. Axiom-man never said a word to me. Just acted. Broke my ribs, my arm, then left me there to listen to the whole thing. Oh those poor kids."*

Captain Jack Gunn of the Special Force Unit was working around the clock, the article said, and despite statements to assure the public everything was all right, it went on to say any sighting of Axiom-man should be reported immediately.

Heart aching, Gabriel set down his bowl, his appetite gone.

"I got to stop this guy."

He wondered why the article had ran. If Jack was doing a manhunt, Gabriel thought such an operation would be kept secret so the cops could get the jump on him, but at the same time, notifying the public meant the WPD and SFU had eyes and ears everywhere. How many people would have the courage to phone in an

Axiom-man sighting remained to be seen if they thought he had suddenly become dangerous.

*After all this time, after all I've done—thought I would've proven myself. Look how quickly it's become undone.* The scariest part was not that everyone was looking for him.

It was that this imposter was still out there.

————

At seventy-three, Helen had no choice but to undergo a hip replacement after a nasty fall last winter. The recovery after surgery had been agonizing and for some reason her body wouldn't co-operate with her during the therapy afterward. As time went on and mobility slowly returned, she decided not to let another moment pass without reclaiming parts of her life she had once held dear: she resumed bowling, and had been doing so at least once a week for the past three months. She'd loved the game growing up, even played it with her husband while they dated and even into the first few years of their marriage. As childrearing took over, she got too busy for the sport and, as more time went on, kept setting it aside in favor of friend and family commitments.

As she sat in the back of the Handi-Transit minivan, she wished her husband could play one last game with her. Unfortunately, Armand was well into his eighties and dementia had set in some years back. Even when she visited him at the nursing home he barely recognized her and when he did, he wasn't sure what year it was.

She sat in traffic, the Handi-Transit driver, Ryan, making small talk, the usual bits about the weather and the whole "how's your grandkids?" thing. Nothing of substance, and Helen was still trying to figure out why people talked to seniors as if they were children, all slow and with simple words.

"I might be seventy-three, but I'm not an idiot," she'd said to more than one person who spoke to her that way. The other person would get on the defensive when she pointed out the disrespect since most seniors didn't say anything and just took being spoken to like a child as part of "growing old." It was nonsense and Helen stood by that.

Traffic was especially thick today and she wondered what was going on. Then again, this was Winnipeg and if traffic wasn't backed up by rush hour, then it could only mean it was by construction.

The minivan suddenly rocked and the driver honked his horn. With a loud crash, a blue-gloved fist punched through the driver's side window, striking Ryan in the side of the head. He fell over, dazed, blood oozing from his cut cheek and ear.

"Ryan?" she asked.

The vehicle rocked again and the cars surrounding them in traffic honked. Some people yelled. The vehicle lurched one final time and the whole thing became airborne.

Helen peered out the window and didn't see anything. How was the minivan flying?

"Help! Ryan, wake up!"

He groaned and righted himself. "What the—" He looked out the window, let out a yelp, then laid on the horn.

Its blare hurt Helen's ears. "Ryan, do something!" she shouted above its sound.

They were over the bridge, at least a hundred feet up. The river ran beneath the bridge and the minivan started over in that direction.

"Help! Somebody, help!" Ryan screamed out the window.

Helen's stomach suddenly left its spot and rose into her throat as the minivan fell from the air and plummeted to the river below. The whole thing violently jolted as it made impact, so much so her and Ryan jerked within their seat belts; the agonizing pain of her hip and the artificial one breaking inside her made her squeal. Her head snapped forward and back and something cracked at the base of her skull.

Dazed and sick to her stomach, she screamed for help as water poured into the smashed window beside Ryan. He only groaned.

As the vehicle filled with muddy brown water, Helen's heart did a little dance when she saw Axiom-man fly down level with the water in front of the vehicle.

"Help! In here! Help!" she screamed.

Axiom-man pried open the roof above Ryan's seat, tore the seat belt off him as if tearing paper, then pulled Ryan out.

"Hey, what about me?" she screamed.

The opening Axiom-man created in the roof let the water in full force and the vehicle was quickly pulled under. As the cold water engulfed her, she screamed against it one more time and started saying her prayers when she realized she'd taken in a lungful of water and Axiom-man wasn't coming back for her.

Her last thought was a replay of that blue-gloved fist smashing the window and her knowing he had caused what just happened. She shuddered to think what he was doing to Ryan right now.

As the sunlight filtering through the water's surface faded from view, she thought of Armand and wondered if her husband would notice she wouldn't be visiting anymore.

———

"Two bucks a ticket and this ride costs three of them?" Jodie said. "Are you kidding me? He's only four!"

Parking lot carnivals were many things and cheap wasn't one of them.

"Fine. Whatever," she said and handed the tickets over. The guy took them with a smug look that read he knew full well she was being ripped off. But anything for Mikey, even an over-priced Ferris Wheel ride.

While they waited in line, Mikey looked up at her. "I can't wait to go real high, Mommy. I'll close my eyes if I get scared."

"Then you won't be able to see me watching you the whole time," she said.

"You're not coming with me?"

"I can't, Mikey, I'm sorry. These tickets are really expensive . . . but that's okay. I'll have fun standing here watching you."

"I'm scared."

"Don't be scared. Be brave."

When it came time for their turn, the man running the machine opened the carriage door and asked to see their stamps.

"Just him," Jodie said and handed him the tickets.

"He can't ride alone," the man replied.

From behind, a squeaky male voice said, "I'll go with him." It was a kid of around fourteen.

"You sure?" Jodie asked.

"Yeah, no problem."

To Mikey, she said, "You go with this young man here. He'll take good care of you."

The teen went ahead and sat down; Mikey hesitantly went with him. When the carriage door closed, Jodie blew her son a kiss and gave him a wave. The expression on Mikey's face went from trepidation to excitement in a matter of seconds and when the carriage started moving, he was all smiles.

Jodie stepped back and watched as the carriage went up and up and up, and soon Mikey was at the top. When he came back down and around he waved, a big smile on his face going ear-to-ear. It was so good to see him enjoying himself. She had been so busy working these past few weeks, and between going to and from her job and dropping off and picking up Mikey from nursery and daycare, she had hardly spent any time with him, as by the time they got home, he had to be off to bed.

She watched as the carriage went round and round before settling near the top while the guy running the Ferris Wheel let off a couple of riders and let on two more, these ones a young couple who were a little too touchy-feely for Jodie's tastes. With a violent jerk, the whole Ferris Wheel lurched and she looked up at Mikey. His carriage rocked side-to-side like the others. The teen sitting beside him peered out between the carriage bars.

By another carriage near the top beside the supports was . . . Axiom-man. He pressed against the carriage beams and bent the metal with his gloved hands. The people inside screamed and pleaded for him to stop. The metal creaked and groaned before snapping loose and the carriage went tumbling off, flipping and turning, spiraling into the ground below. The bodies burst within the cages like jam-filled rag dolls on impact.

Jodie's mouth went wide, but no sound escaped as she tried to scream.

Axiom-man was at Mikey's carriage and doing the same thing. The man in blue pressed against the metal supports. They creaked and groaned from the pressure of his hands.

Mikey shrieked and the teen inside yelled expletives, begging Axiom-man to stop. When Axiom-man didn't, the teen tried reaching through the openings in the carriage's frame and swung his fists out at Axiom-man. He was too far away and couldn't land a hit. Mikey pulled on the teen's shirt, pulled and pulled and pulled. Her little boy looked down at her and the tears filling her eyes blurred him from vision. She wiped her eyes only to have them immediately fill up again.

"Not Mikey!" she screamed. "Not my baby!"

The metal bars popped and groaned as Axiom-man pushed against them.

The teen inside the carriage was white with fear, but managed to put his arm around Mikey and hold him close as the support beams snapped and the carriage went tumbling to the ground.

Jodie didn't know whose screams were louder: hers . . . or Mikey's.

# Chapter Six

*YOU'D THINK THAT guy would have a little sympathy,* Gabriel thought as he left the unemployment office. The man he'd dealt with had been all business, no smiles, and all he cared about, it seemed, was not offering any suggestions to help him find soon employment, just that the right forms were filled out.

Gabriel slowly moved his head ear to shoulder, stretching the muscles. His neck was still sore and it felt more joint-related than muscle-based. He'd only been to a chiropractor once when he was a kid after sleeping at a weird angle one night and waking up unable to turn his head to the left. He hoped it would only take one visit to right whatever wrong that uppercut had done to him.

As he walked the sidewalks downtown, he glanced at the people, thinking that each one was potentially on the lookout for Axiom-man and little did they realize the guy in glasses and collared shirt walking among them was the man they were looking for.

It did bring up an interesting question: what he was going to do about laying low. He couldn't just shirk his Axiom-man duties and let other people suffer for it, yet he couldn't fly around in his gear without people inevitably spotting him. A temporary costume until all this blew over, maybe? He wasn't in the mood to sew something new nor had the funds to pay for the materials to do so. Maybe he had something lying around at home he could quickly piece together and use in the meantime? People might put two and two together once they saw someone else doing the things Axiom-man could, but maybe by the time it dawned on them, even if just a few seconds later, it could be enough time to flee the scene and move on to the next thing.

Gabriel passed by a hotdog stand, the scent of the all-beef wieners making his stomach growl. He had a weak spot for street dogs and it was tempting to shell out the four bucks for just one.

*No, got to conserve,* he told himself.

As he passed by the cart, the vendor had the radio on and something by the Hip was playing. He couldn't remember the name of the song. Or maybe it was a new one. Being so busy with work and being a superhero had put him out of touch with a lot of things, music being one of them.

It could've been his low mood over losing his job, or knowing someone was out there destroying everything Axiom-man stood for, but when his stomach growled a third time, he decided he deserved to cut himself a break. Besides, the unemployment insurance was most likely going to go through so it wasn't like he was completely out of cash never mind his upcoming severance pay.

Yeah, he could afford the four bucks. Kind of.

He stood in line and could already taste that juicy dog complete with ketchup, mustard, onions, a few hot peppers and—

The female radio DJ spoke up as the Hip faded away. *". . . Ferris Wheel in a parking lot fair over on McLeod and Gateway. Passengers from seven carriages were sent tumbling to their deaths today as Axiom-man broke them off the wheel. Those looking on stood in shock and awe as the once-famed superhero went on a killing spree. Casualties included adults, teens and children. Spokesman for the Winnipeg Police, Matthew Shaw, said a citywide manhunt is already underway and that anyone with any knowledge as to Axiom-man's whereabouts should contact 911 immediately, where they will be patched through to the Special Force*

*Unit, who will take over the matter."* The woman paused and when she spoke again, her voice cracked, as if she was holding back tears. *"I don't know what to make of this. I thought . . . I don't normally voice personal opinion on the air, but I hope Axiom-man burns in Hell for what he's done. I . . ."* The radio went silent for a moment before an ad from Winnipeg Honda came on.

It was Gabriel's turn to order.

"What'll it be, man?" the portly hotdog vendor asked.

"Nothing," he said, losing his appetite for the second time that day.

---

Valerie Vaughan sat at her reception desk near the top floor of the eighty-storey Owen Tower. She'd seen the news.

Axiom-man had gone rogue.

Why? Had it become too much for him and he just snapped? So many encounters with death, pain and those who would do the city harm . . . did they finally wear him down and something gave way?

"Gabriel . . ." she said softly. "How could you?"

Her heart raced as she realized she could put a stop to the madness right away. It would only take one phone call to the police. She could tell them who Axiom-man really was, tell them all she knew: his real name, his phone number, address, where he worked—everything.

*Then why don't you?* she wondered. *Is it because you care, or is it because you're afraid he'll come after you* when *he finds out you betrayed him? He's not stupid. You're the only one who knows who he really is. He'd put two and two together in no time.*

She glanced at the phone. A part of her wanted to call him and wondered if he was home. After those men had kidnapped her when the city was under Bleaken's control, and after Axiom-man rescued her, she had undergone weeks of trauma counseling. They wanted her to write out everything that happened, not sparing a single detail. She did, the only thing omitted Axiom-man visiting her in the hospital room afterward. It was there she called him by his real name, revealing she knew who he was.

She was surprised he didn't react to it. It was almost like he either knew that she knew already, or was simply at total peace with it and it didn't spark a reaction.

Valerie couldn't see him after that. Not anymore. Not after those men hurt her and Axiom-man came crashing in and beat that man within an inch of his life. The rage he exuded as he laid into her captor. Had she not told him to stop, she feared he would've kept going all because of his feelings toward her. Was that a precursor to what was happening now? Had Gabriel flipped because *she* rejected him?

But it wasn't rejection. It was about distancing. It was about being safe.

It was about stepping back after so many close calls with those with special abilities.

She couldn't handle it anymore.

But what was happening now and all those people dying . . . . She glanced at the phone again.

Valerie didn't know who to call: Gabriel or the police.

---

Getting a same-day appointment with a chiropractor was a blessing and Gabriel felt so much better as he walked out of the doctor's office. He was a bit achy, but while he was there he asked for a complete head-to-toe adjustment, emphasis on his neck injury. He'd been warned he might be sore for a day or two following, but should be feeling a whole lot better afterward and was to make a follow-up appointment for a few days from now. Gabriel decided he'd play it by ear instead and see how he was feeling. The injury to his neck, it turned out, wasn't as severe as he thought.

The plan was to go home and find something he could suit up in other than his Axiom-man costume, then hit the skies and fly over every street and try to find the guy imitating him. He just hoped whoever it was was out and about so he could locate them, but yet that also ran the risk of this person being out there because they were going to kill again. After hearing about that Ferris Wheel incident, Gabriel resolved to deal with this person quickly and with enough force to not only subdue them, but keep them down for good.

When he got home, he dug around in his closet and pulled out dark gray sweatpants, a matching hoodie, and his winter gloves. He'd wear work boots on his feet. For his face . . . he rummaged around his closet some more and found a black neck warmer. Between the hood drawn tight, the neck warmer over his mouth and his eyes glowing blue, his identity would be kept a secret. Gabriel had a feeling of déjà vu as cobbling together this outfit reminded him of when he had just received his powers and was experimenting with them prior to creating his Axiom-man suit. There was something homey about it that encouraged his heart he was still on the right path and that Axiom-man was who he was meant to be, something he could know for himself and not because the messenger told him so.

Stomach growling, the day's scant eating caught up with him and he was quickly nauseous. Opting for a heated can of fried beans mixed with a can of Alphagetti, he prepped his meal, wolfed it down and followed it up with a tall glass of milk. Once the food started making its way through his system he'd perk right up and be ready for whatever the evening might bring.

———

Jeremy was grateful for the meal. He had missed the cut-off time at the shelter for last night's dinner after losing track of time pan-handling downtown. He had missed the cut-off for breakfast this morning, too, thanks to sleeping in, and was too far away come lunch time. It wasn't like him to do that. He usually had the schedule down pat and was able to get his three squares a day without fail. After all, he had been doing it since finding himself stuck on the streets since the tail end of winter.

The company he'd been working for had folded. He had a good thing going with them. Great salary, benefits, the whole nine yards. He'd made a good buck and spent a good buck. Spent too many of them, and when the market took a dive and the company had overextended itself on a few projects, even what was in the company's reserves wasn't enough to keep it afloat. Jeremy, along with the other eighty-nine people who worked there, suddenly found themselves without a job. He'd tried going on unemployment, but between the mix ups and the folks he was dealing with giving him a hard time— could've been because he'd cussed them out more than once—his claim was never processed and the payments on the house, the car, the big screen, the pool never mind his overdue credit cards all went unmet. He'd tried making arrangements for his bills, asking friends for money—but trying to double the handouts he received at the casino backfired and eventually he lost everything.

Tonight the shelter was serving meatball soup. He'd never had it before but was so hungry he didn't care. Being on the street taught him to be thankful for the little he had—the clothes on his back, his three squares, the cash he was saving up from begging—even so far as using some of that money to help out others who were even worse off than he was. He never spent it though. It was meant for getting back on his feet when the time was right.

Things were turning around—slowly—but turning around nonetheless and he knew that once he was back on his feet, he'd be a better person for what happened.

He found a quiet spot at the end of the corner table; quiet not for nobody being there—the place was pretty full—but Mark and Tyler never talked much so he knew he'd be getting a meal alone with his thoughts.

The soup was amazing, the meatballs juicy, flavorful, and had he been much of a cook, he would've asked for the recipe.

With a loud bang that sent a jolt through Jeremy's chest, the door's blew open and two bodies went flying across the room, crashing into the serving station beyond, spilling hot soup all over the volunteers behind it. Jeremy looked to see Axiom-man stride in, shoulders back, as if he owned the place. A couple guys put up their fists and after a few seconds of sizing up the man in the blue cape, they made a move on him. Axiom-man simply grabbed them, lifted them off their feet, and hurled them across the room. He picked up the nearest table, including the people sitting at it on the attached bench. He hoisted the whole thing over his head and threw it against the wall, the unit landing as such that it slammed against the people attached to it, squishing them as drywall tumbled down, revealing the dense wooden frame and insulation beyond. They, and the broken table, crashed to the ground.

Jeremy jumped from his seat.

Mark threw his bowl of soup at Axiom-man. The ceramic bowl smashed against the side of Axiom-man's head, covering him in gooey balls of ground beef. Axiom-man looked over at Mark and, with a yell, leaped across the room in one shot, grabbed him by the collar, and threw him through the window. Mark's scream faded then was silenced when he smashed into something on the other side out on the street.

Tyler took a swing and Axiom-man blocked it, grabbed his arm, broke it, then punched his fingers into Tyler's throat and ripped out his trachea. A bit of bile rose in Jeremy's throat and his legs turned to rubber, giving out completely. He sunk to the floor.

A couple of other guys jumped on Axiom-man from the back. The man in blue flipped one over his shoulder, slamming him to the ground. The other guy he pulled off him as if it was nothing, like peeling off a piece of stray tape. He tore the guy's arm from his body then dug both hands into the bloody shoulder socket and snapped his hands out to either side, ripping the guy in two.

The scream came out uncontrollably and no matter how hard Jeremy tried to shut himself up, he couldn't stifle his voice. Axiom-man came over to him and the last thing Jeremy saw were two fingers coming for his eyes. Pain exploded inside his skull as his eyes were pushed into his head, then fire lit the sockets and his cheekbones as he was hoisted by them off his feet. The next impact was a slam to his chest. He heard the ribs break on the left side and when warmth flooded the same area while blood gushed out, he knew Axiom-man had just ripped his heart from his body.

# CHAPTER SEVEN

THE INTERNET WAS abuzz with comments of Axiom-man having lost it.

Oscar Owen smiled. He sat checking his phone at the Keg, his steak dinner already ordered.

*It's all starting to fall apart for him. At least the police have stepped up and are making efforts to bring him in. It won't be long until escalation fully takes hold and Axiom-man won't be able to set a boot anywhere without someone coming after him.*

A text came in pertaining to the grand opening of Owen Tower. He answered it, and confirmed he'd review the guest list one final time and get back to his assistant, who'd in turn get in touch with the appropriate parties and verify the presence of some of the city's most important people.

Back to the news, an incident at one of the city's shelter's had the police worried and Oscar wondered if they'd initiate a curfew to help keep the citizens safe.

*Won't stop any damage from being done. Not at the rate this is going.*

The waitress approached his table, tray of food in hand. She set it down before him and he couldn't wait to get going on it. Everyone loved a good steak.

Especially a rare one.

---

Suited up in his new "costume," Axiom-man flew through the sky, staying true to his plan of flying over every street, eyes on the lookout for the imposter. It'd been several hours and he'd found nothing, but he was determined to stay out all night if he had to. Wasn't like he had a job to go to in the morning anymore.

A car alarm went off somewhere down the block. Axiom-man sped over. Below, a couple of young guys were running away from a flashing vehicle. Axiom-man landed beside the Lexus. The window was smashed, a brick on the seat.

"Punks," he said. *So many more important things going on and you're going to waste my time with this?*

He flew off the ground, over the two teenagers running away, and landed on the other side of them.

"Think you're going to owe the owner of that car an apology," Axiom-man said.

"Yo, man, who are you? How'd you do that?" the one guy said.

"I'm—" *As if you don't know.*

The other guy spoke up. "Yo, man, what's up with his eyes?" To Axiom-man, "Think we should teach you some manners." He reached into his pocket and pulled out a knife.

"Put that away," Axiom-man said.

"Or what?"

"Or I'll make you put it away."

The guy's eyes lit up with anger. "Yeah?" He moved in with a wild slash. Axiom-man moved to the side, grabbed the wrist, and squeezed. A bone rotated out of place beneath his thumb. The guy hollered in pain and dropped the knife. Axiom-man pulled him to the ground and the other guy jumped on him and started raining blows on his back. Axiom-man hit the pavement on his hands and knees. Each thud from the guy's bony fists sent a jolt of pain through his shoulder blades. He threw his elbows back in quick succession, catching the guy in the ribs and sending him off him. He wasn't sure if he broke them or not, though with his ultra strength, it would've been easy to do.

Before he could get back up, the guy jumped onto him again. Axiom-man rolled over, keeping the guy beneath him. When the teen wrapped his legs around him, he used the side of his fists and gave the guy a wicked Charlie horse on each thigh. The guy yelped and his legs quickly relaxed. Axiom-man rolled over, faced him square on, and socked him one.

"Stay down!" Axiom-man said.

The guy turtled, whimpering, whatever bravado clearly sucked out of him.

His friend came in from behind, the knife back in hand. Axiom-man moved out of the way just as the guy came in and redirected the blade so it wouldn't strike the other kid. With a quick hard hook to the jaw, he put the guy out.

Both teens lay on the ground, the one still whimpering.

*I have to call this in*, he thought. *Can't let them see me, though, as they'll see my new—these guys will describe me anyway. Will have to pretend to be a concerned citizen, nothing more.*

He produced a couple zip-ties from his pocket and tied up the teens. The car alarm finally shut off and, down the street, he saw who he presumed was the car's owner standing next to it.

The guy came running down the street in shorts and a tank top. He was holding something but Axiom-man couldn't see what it was from this far away.

"Hey, you!" the guy shouted.

When the guy caught up, Axiom-man said, "These guys dropped a brick on your front seat. Might want to look into pressing charges."

The guy—probably around thirty or so, short black hair, muscular—had a dopey grin on his face.

"What?" Axiom-man said.

The guy lifted his gun and pointed it at Axiom-man. He pulled out a police-issue walkie-talkie from the back of his shorts. "Suspect in front of me. He took the bait."

"This is a setup?"

"Didn't take much. I'll give you credit for trying to stop the little things. Nice outfit, by the way. Don't know how you thought it would fool us."

A handful of uniformed police officers emerged from behind fences and ran out to the street, all with their weapons drawn.

Axiom-man knew if he tried to take off, they'd open fire and there was no way he was fast enough to outfly a bullet. He wasn't sure how he could talk himself out of this one either.

Sirens rang and flashing red and blue lights appeared down the street. Another bigger vehicle followed it and when it got closer he recognized it as belonging to the Special Force Unit. Jack was on the way.

"Take off the mask, man," the guy said.

"I don't think your captain would be too happy with you asking that. I think that's something he'd want for himself." He was bluffing, obviously. Jack had already seen him without his mask in the Tireland warehouse that time with Katie. Fortunately, his eyes had been swollen after taking a beating and concealed the shape of his face never mind the bruising, acting like a natural mask.

The sirens grew louder and the SFU pulled up. Sure enough, Jack hopped out of the passenger seat and came running over. He came up beside the guy in the tank top. "I got it, but keep a weapon on him."

"Hi, Jack," Axiom-man said, flat.

"Don't 'hi' me. There's no disaster around here to take you away from me this time."

"I told you, it wasn't me."

"Then why are you dressed like that? Think you could fool us?"

"Think I'd even come out knowing you're looking for me? Good job on the sting. Either you knew I'd be doing my job too well, or you took a big risk by getting a couple of kids involved. They should get looked at by someone, by the way."

"They're dead?"

"Hurt. They attacked me."

To the guy in the tank top, Jack said, "Go check up on them, make sure this guy didn't do anything to them that's permanent." To Axiom-man: "Now I got you on assault, too."

"You can't. I met them with equal force, self-defence."

"We'll see."

*We're wasting time.* Axiom-man raised his hands in surrender in a gesture of goodwill. "Look, you take me in and the madness won't stop."

"Is that a threat?"

"It's not me, Jack!" he shouted. "You're so stubborn. Listen, you don't believe me, then you'll see for yourself I'm telling the truth when the next group of people die."

"That better not be a threat," he muttered. Louder: "If I take you in, no one's going to die."

"You're not listening to me."

"No, you're not listening to me! You brought a serious threat upon this city just by being here. First Redsaw, then Bleaken and—"

"I stopped those guys."

"Now stop yourself."

"It's not me." Axiom-man glanced around. All the cops still had their guns on him. There was no way out of this. "I'm not going with you."

"Yes, you are."

Axiom-man gritted his teeth. The surrounding cops began to close in and Jack pulled out a pair of handcuffs from his belt. These weren't standard issue, either. They were much thicker. Did Jack think they'd hold him? Maybe, depending what they were made of and how much force it'd take to break the metal.

*He's left me no choice. If I don't save myself, the killer will still be out there. Having me get put away is what the imposter wants. Whether that means he stops killing after I'm gone, I don't know, and if he does, the city is left wide open.* Axiom-man filled up his eyes with blue energy.

"Everybody, look out!" Jack shouted.

Axiom-man let loose and fired off an energy blast at one of the cars parked on the side of the road. The vehicle exploded, creating a deafening boom that made some of the officers gasp and everyone either duck or take cover.

Axiom-man immediately flew straight up, going as fast as he could. Gunshots went off beneath him and he heard the whiz of the bullets as they cut through the air around him. His dark clothing would quickly help him blend in with the night sky the higher he flew. Sure enough, after about ten seconds, the shots stopped.

*Now I just started a war with the police*, he thought. *Great.*

Several thousand feet up, he angled himself to level out and slow down . . . but he couldn't.

He started flying faster.

# CHAPTER EIGHT

THE WIND RUSHING past Axiom-man's ears blocked out any other sound. He tried turning over to the right and left, even forward and backward—anything to get himself parallel to the ground. Instead he kept racing upward, flying at a speed that shoved air into his mouth faster than his lungs could take in.

The cold air blew hard against the exposed areas of his face and he knew if he didn't level out soon, the air would grow too cold and too thin, and he'd be a goner.

*What's going on?* he thought, then a moment later flashed to the last time he lost control of his powers: *A . . . what did the messenger call it? A spike? A push? A . . . surge! Yeah, a surge!* His panicking heart rate slowed a little at the thought that this spike in power should level out soon, if a surge was indeed what it was. How soon, though, he didn't know and if it didn't happen quickly, it wouldn't matter because he'd be dead.

Lungs starting to hurt for lack of air, Axiom-man ground his teeth and bit back the pain, focusing on just toughing it out until it was over. Maybe his powers would cut out if he lost consciousness? If they did, he'd quickly start falling to his death and unless he awoke before hitting the ground . . .

The air suddenly took a sharp dip in temperature and the skin on his forehead started to freeze along with even the skin beneath the neck warmer covering his mouth.

A bright blue haze of energy filtered over his eyes and he sensed its tingling power not only covering his eyes, but leaking out and slowly encompassing his face, down his neck, chest and, soon, his entire body. The crackle and pop of its powerful energy snapped around his ears, a few of them even louder than the rush of wind blowing past.

Lungs burning for oxygen, he tried to scream but the air crashing against his face as he rapidly ascended forbade any sound from coming out.

The light around him grew bright, at first a light blue, to a fierce electric blue, to nearly white, and then with a loud crack, a bright burst of blinding white light shot before his eyes and his flight finally began to slow. Not only that, air flooded into his lungs, triggering a coughing fit. When he regained his composure, he felt himself still rising up but the filter of white over his eyes remained, casting everything in a bright glow, even himself. Through the haze of light he saw a faint aura surrounding his body, licks of energy dancing and crackling around him. Its electric power tingled against his skin even through his clothes.

"How am I breathing?" he whispered. The ground was so far below that he couldn't make out anything. Even the city lights were all meshed together.

He was still rising.

Stunned, it didn't dawn on him to try and stop himself until he started to crack the Earth's atmosphere. When he finally did stop, the bright haze of white over his eyes began to fade, first to electric blue then bright blue, then gone altogether though he sensed whatever that aura was hadn't left him completely. His skin still tingled.

His mouth fell open at the sight of the glow of the atmosphere around the Earth, the planet's curve, the stark contrast of its blue against the pitch black of space.

Eyes wide, unblinking, he started to shake from the rush, the adrenaline, the sight.

"I'm . . . I'm . . ." All he could do was smile as his eyes filled with tears at the awesome sight of the Earth meeting space. He wiped his eyes and looked around. The moon was there albeit far away, as well were a few stars very far off. The sun was just over the horizon on the opposite side of the Earth, its brilliant brightness making him instinctively squint.

A surge of vigor bubbled through him and he recognized it as the aftereffects of the surge. If he remembered the last time a surge happened, it was power-specific, with a spike in output pertaining to a particular ability before that same ability settled back down in a stronger way than before. But this time, it seemed, *two* abilities had surged; his flight speed and the energy beams from his eyes.

His skin still tingled beneath his clothes. "What's this, though?" He pulled off his glove and a faint blue glow hovered a scant millimetre from his skin. It was barely perceptible, but it was there. A new power? An expansion of an old one? He didn't know, but he did know of one person who would.

He needed to talk to the messenger.

But not before seeing how fast he could fly.

Axiom-man replaced his glove and again took in the awe-inspiring sight of the planet at the edge of the vastness of space.

So incredible.

Not wanting to leave, but knowing he had to, he took a deep breath to slow his racing heart then dove forward, arms outstretched, and sped back toward the Earth. He noticed an immediate increase in speed. Before, he'd been able to do around eighty kliks an hour. Now . . . he was pushing much more, maybe even double that. He was moving so fast it felt like he would lose control if he wasn't careful. This new speed would definitely take some practice and getting used to. Not only that, but something else was different. Normally, the rush of air slamming into his face from going so fast would make breathing difficult and he'd have to keep his head down and block the wind with the top of his head to help. Now he could face forward no problem and breathe just fine.

*Maybe that glow is protecting me from the outside elements?* he thought. *Is it always there or do I need to be flying?* It had been present when he had been floating above the Earth so, it seemed, he didn't need to hit a certain speed to activate it.

Speed.

Axiom-man smiled beneath his neck warmer as he tore through the air, his body moving at a rate he'd never known before. This was more thrilling than any rollercoaster or death drop he'd ever been on. More thrilling than even the first time he discovered he could fly.

Despite all that was going on, in spite of getting shot at tonight and nearly being captured by the police, Axiom-man couldn't help but laugh as he ripped through the air, the night sky clouds a blur beneath him.

---

Valerie lay awake in bed, tapping her toes together beneath the covers as the seconds ticked by. Though she hoped it was only her imagination, a part of her wondered that if Gabriel had indeed snapped, if he'd come for her at some point. What he would do to her, she didn't know and fought every notion of violence that popped into her mind.

She clung to the fact he cared so much for her and that whatever this was that was going on, at the very least his feelings for her would prevent him from doing anything rash. At the same time, it was a well-documented fact those whom violent aggressors professed to love were always in the most danger.

*I hope not,* she thought. She rolled over onto her side and clung to the covers tight.

---

Axiom-man had to buckle down on his own self-control and put a stop to all the fun after about an hour. It could've been all the stress working itself out, which was why he kept up exploring this new speed for so long, but, frankly, he needed the break. Between an imposter going around killing people, Valerie chucking him, any positive affiliation he had with Jack Gunn out the window, never mind Katie's warning that Jack wasn't to be trusted—he needed to unplug and was ashamed of himself at how un-hero-like that was. He should've still been searching for the imposter instead of playing around. At the same time, taking a time out for himself helped clear his head and made him ready to keep going. Also, if anything, learning to harness this new speed could only help him—and, in turn, help others—going forward.

Above the city streets, Axiom-man had to slow down so he could get a good look at what was going on below. There was some traffic, a few people walking around, but nothing out of the ordinary.

He admitted to himself a slight reluctance to get involved with any minor crimes he spotted solely because he wanted to avoid police presence at all costs. Yet, by the time the cops would get there—if they were called and if it wasn't a setup—he'd be long gone.

He flew past a bus stop on William and saw a scuffle inside one of the bus shelters. Three people. Two big, one small. The police station wasn't far from here either.

With a sigh, he flew down and saw a couple of roughnecks hassling a young woman with long brown hair. She kept trying to step around them to get out of the shelter but they blocked her at every turn, making rude comments.

With a quick stride, Axiom-man walked into the bus shelter and pulled the first guy away.

"She leaves with me," he said. *That's kind of lame. Whatever.*

A look of relief washed over the woman's face.

The other guy gave her a shove, sending her flying into the shelter wall.

"Hey!" Axiom-man said.

"Back off, punk," the first guy said.

"I'm taking her out of here," Axiom-man said and stepped toward the woman. He knew full well the men would attack him but he wasn't about to sit here and negotiate with them, not with the police station nearby and a patrol car that would no doubt be around soon.

The first guy came out swinging. Axiom-man kicked him in the gut and sent him flying across the shelter, where he bounced off the inside wall and hit the ground, holding his stomach.

The second came in with a wide swing. Axiom-man ducked under it then brought his hand to the guy's throat, applied enough pressure to get a good grip, then dragged him across the shelter to the wall next to his friend. He slammed him against it so hard the guy dropped, stunned.

Axiom-man held out his hand to the woman. "Come with me."

She took his hand without hesitation, and he escorted her out.

"You okay?" he asked.

She nodded.

"Did they hurt you?" He glanced at the two men inside the shelter, who lay groaning on the ground.

"A little, but I'll be okay."

"Need me to take you to the doctor? HSC isn't far from here."

"I'll be all right. Thanks."

"Come on," he said, taking her by the arm, "let's get going." He escorted her around the corner and further down the block where he kept his eyes open for any cop cars. Seeing none, he walked with her to the nearest bus stop. "Hope you can still catch your bus from here."

She checked the route numbers on the sign. "Should be able to."

There was a chance those guys in the shelter would recover and track her down, so he said, "I'll wait with you."

They stood in silence, the woman cradling her elbows. He kept a couple of feet back, constantly on the lookout for any cops. After a while, she said, "I know who you are" —she made a circle around her face with her index finger— "beneath that." For a moment he thought she knew who he *really*-really was, then understood she meant who he was beneath the pseudo-costume. "I also know what the paper says about you. The whole city is talking. Is it true?"

Quietly, he asked, "Do you think it is?"

She studied him, furrowing her brow. She shook her head. "No. I think someone's out to get you. If you really were a killer, you wouldn't have saved me."

He couldn't believe what he was about to say, but the words just kind of came out. "What if I wanted to get you away from them so I could have you to myself?"

"Not with the way you touched my arm. I could feel the gentleness. Trust me, I've been around some bad dudes before and there was always an edge to them even when they tried to be tender. I could feel the genuine care for my wellbeing through your touch. I mean, unless you've practiced pretending to be one thing when you're really another so well, I knew I'd be safe." She choked a bit on those last words.

Little did she realize she wasn't far from the truth. He *had* lots of practice of pretending to be someone he wasn't, just not in the way she meant.

She cleared her throat. "Do you know who's impersonating you?"

"No. I've thought about it, but I don't have much to go on. I'm trying to find him, though." A Transit appeared further down the street. Axiom-man nodded toward it. "Is this you?"

She glanced at the bus. "Yeah. Thank you, again."

"You're welcome."

He waited with her until the bus was almost at the stop then turned away so the bus driver wouldn't see his glowing eyes and possibly call it in.

She got on and he walked away. When the bus was further down the street and he was out of view of anyone within, his feet left the ground and he rose into the sky.

# CHAPTER NINE

THE NEXT MORNING, Gabriel sat in front of his computer, coffee in hand, scanning the headlines. A nursing home had been hit last night. Twenty-six seniors were not only dead, but each one disemboweled. Axiom-man had been caught on tape ripping them to pieces. Gabriel wished he could somehow get a copy of it and, as awful as it would be, watch the guy in action so he could maybe find out more behind who was impersonating him.

He thought back to the surge last night. The power he had felt running through him when the whole thing was at its peak was stunning, and afterward, it really did seem like his flight speed had doubled. The last time he spoke to him, the messenger had said these surges would happen as Gabriel used his powers, the very use of his abilities making them grow stronger, which would eventually manifest all in one shot now and then. This strange aura, however, he wasn't sure about. He didn't know if it would remain as it was, or if it would eventually become stronger itself and be this bright blue glow around his body, or what it was for other than, thus far, proving to protect him from the inherent hazards of flying.

Even this morning he had *shifted* to see if the aura was still there and it was, very faint, covering his body head-to-toe. It wasn't noticeable through his clothing as it remained directly on his skin.

It was pretty cool though.

Gabriel took a sip of coffee and hoped the caffeine would start working its magic soon. It'd been a late night again after helping that woman. There had been a convenience store robbery but the perpetrators had fled by the time he got there and the man working the counter was in the process of calling the cops. Gabriel wasn't sure if the man put two and two together and realized the guy with the glowing blue eyes coming in to help was Axiom-man or not. He didn't want to stick around to find out, though. Elsewhere, a cabbie had the taxi's external emergency light on, signaling distress within the car. Gabriel had put a stop to the assault while the cabbie sustained minor injury. The assailant, however, not so much, not after he tried taking Gabriel to the ground.

A new headline popped into his inbox. When he opened it, it was an official police statement via the *Free Press* stating they were going to redouble their efforts to catch Axiom-man, especially after the famed superhero attacked the cops last night. Add that to the nursing home incident and they were ticked.

"There's probably going to be a curfew," Gabriel said. "People aren't going to be happy and are going to take it out on Axiom-man if it comes into effect. I know folks were real mad the last time a crisis happened and they were told to stay indoors, even though it was for their own safety." He thought back to Redsaw's rampage throughout the city and all murders he executed before the Doorway opened, and when Bleaken had covered the city in a black cloud. "They might even extend it to the day time. Would shut the whole city down, if that happened. Whoever this guy is, this has to end. I just don't know how to find him."

Gabriel sat staring at the keyboard, not really focusing on the keys, and let his mind wander. He needed the messenger. Not only to tell him about the surge, but perhaps the messenger knew how to locate the Axiom-man imposter or, even, who he was.

The problem was, it wasn't like the messenger had a contact number. He just kind of showed up.

---

Valerie sat at her desk at work, drumming her fingers next to her keyboard. When Oscar Owen appeared behind the opening elevator doors, she quickly put her fingers on the keys and pretended like she was doing something. The man had been so impressed with her as his receptionist at the Owen Tower temp office while the tower was being built, he kept her on as his executive assistant. Not only did she man the front desk near the top floor of the high-rise, but also ran him special errands, took letters, and made personal arrangements for him. The job also came with a generous raise so while it wasn't her first career choice, it was too good an opportunity to pass up.

"Morning," Oscar said as he strode past her desk. His black hair was parted neatly to the side, his gray eyes always piercing. The charcoal Brioni suit he wore brought out his broad shoulders and she felt her eyes lingering on him more than she meant to. He wasn't really her type but the more she worked with him, the more she got used to him and noticed how striking he was.

"Morning."

"I have a few private calls to make this morning so I won't be taking general calls until this afternoon," he said.

"Understood."

"Also sent you the finalized guest list for the opening. Please confirm those we've already asked to attend will attend. It's important to this company and for the city that those invited will be there."

"I'll follow up," she said.

He went through the double doors leading into his office and closed them behind him.

She brought up his email and started crosschecking the guest list he sent with the one she had on file. She'd try to get all the calls done by lunch.

Once more, her mind wandered to Gabriel and she was tempted to search the newswires to see if there had been another incident last night.

*Why?* she wondered. *To scare yourself? What if something did happen? You can't let this go on. You know who he is and if he is indeed responsible, you have no choice but to call the cops. You don't want anyone else to die because you didn't say anything. Who knows how many have already died because you waited?*

She went to the search engine and was about to type, but then took her fingers off the keys and pulled her cellphone from her purse. She scanned her address book for Gabriel's number and poised her finger above the touchscreen, ready to dial.

———

Jack Gunn awoke at his desk with a start. When he sat up, he had a report stuck to his face. He peeled it off and his eyes went immediately to the coffee pot. It was down to the bottom line and was in dire need of a refill.

Head aching, he stood, arched his back, stretched, then made a quick trip to the john before coming back and pouring himself a cup of joe. He checked the sugar container and was none too happy when only a small sprinkle came out.

"Hit me when I'm down," he said. He tapped the container over his cup, set it down, then took a much-needed swig. He peeked over his shoulder at the open door. Chatter from the offices beyond wafted down the hallway. He went over to his desk and unlocked the bottom cabinet, pulling out a half bottle of Sailor Jerry's. Best rum on the planet. He added some to his coffee then fumbled with putting it back when footsteps rose in the hallway outside, quickly getting louder. A couple of officers walked past. They'd probably just give him an odd look, if he got caught, but would most likely understand. This thing with Axiom-man had gone too far and what went down at the nursing home was the last straw, never mind Axiom-man nearly killing a couple of his men with that car explosion and then flying away. And to think the man thought he could fool him by not wearing that ridiculous blue costume of his—it'd only be a matter of time before he gave himself away.

The Special Force Unit had been designed for super-powered threats, not only those who made it clear from the start they were on the opposite side of the law, but also those who were supposedly the good guys. Right from the beginning when Axiom-man first came onto the scene, Jack knew it was only a matter of time before containment would be necessary. His assumptions were proven right when Redsaw went from hero to foe and went on a murdering spree throughout the city, proved correct yet again when that Bleaken guy nearly took out all of Winnipeg in a cloud of darkness, then now, with Axiom-man running the streets red with blood—yes, it was time for action.

City funding only went so far and Jack was grateful the Special Force Unit was created as a means to deal with super-powered individuals, but what was the department able to do versus those with such an edge that sometimes even conventional weapons wouldn't make a difference? There was no training for this kind of thing. Even in the theory rooms and endless meetings with government officials, the military and the rest of the WPD, RCMP, private high end security companies—it was all conjecture and review of "what we know." That's why getting the Enhancer was so important. It could at least give his men an edge when combating rogue super-powered individuals. The Enhancer would transform a man into an elite human being, strengthening not only the person's body to peak physical levels, but increasing mental aptitude, emotional strength, will power, learning rate and more. But that all went south at the Tireland fire—Axiom-man and Katianna White to blame—and those above Jack weren't too happy about what happened. To have an enhanced police presence on the streets enabled the government—local, provincial and federal—to gain a modicum of control over these super-powered people and start the process of leveling the playing field.

Jack went along with it because he had no choice. It was either play ball or get a new job. The problem with being an idealist, he supposed. Despite his issues with Axiom-man, he knew the Cobalt Crusader had started out with the right intentions. The problem was now Axiom-man had snapped and people were dying.

The efforts to peaceably bring Axiom-man to justice had failed, everything from reasoning with him to trying to take him in via a group effort.

Now it was time to pull out all the stops.

Now it was time for Operation Rogue.

———

Gabriel had sat by his computer all morning, calling out to the messenger, hoping the strange being could somehow hear him and answer his request. He knew from past experience it wouldn't suddenly make the being of bright blue light appear, but he hoped calling out for him would show initiative—even humility—and demonstrate him doing a good job by asking for help when it was needed.

Instead, he watched as another headline rolled in, this one saying the Greyhound Bus Depot had been hit and over a hundred and fifty riders either pulling up in the buses or waiting to leave in one were killed when the whole building exploded after one bus came crashing through the place, a second hot on its tail then colliding with it.

Gabriel got up, went to his closet and dug around for another outfit since the cops had seen him in the gray-hooded one. He came away with a dark red ski mask and matching track pants and jacket. A pair of black finger mitts and his only pair of sneakers topped the outfit off. It wasn't glamorous, but it was comfortable and would keep his face covered.

He needed to find this guy. The real question was where he would strike next as the targets seemed completely random.

# CHAPTER TEN

TWO DAYS LATER and still not a sign of the Axiom-man imposter. It was evening and Gabriel paced his apartment, exhausted, having spent the better part of each day and night combing the city streets searching for him. Aside from stopping the occasional crime—with a couple of them resulting in those he rescued calling the cops on him—he managed to arrive too late to three separate killing sprees, not to mention the many others he had missed because of having no way of knowing where they'd happen.

He'd never forget ducking under the police tape and walking through that daycare centre and seeing the blood stains on the carpet and walls. Never forget the sounds of trapped people as he tried to dig them out of a collapsed building only to have the police shoot at him and send him off-site. Never forget the sound of the inferno encompassing an entire neighborhood block and the screams of anguish coming from within as people burned alive, the flames too wild and too hot for him to enter and try to save them.

He was out of alternative outfits, too. Any time he was spotted, a description was radioed in. He had a few more he could try, but at best they'd just enable him to walk around at ground level without getting a second glance as long as he kept his glowing eyes hidden, and with everyone looking for him, he'd keep his powers activated so he could use them on a split second's notice, if needed be. Once he was airborne and someone spotted him, it was all over.

He also realized that the clothing was all headed for the trash as well since he didn't want to be wearing it out and about one day, even in partial, and have someone recognize the clothes and think maybe the young man with brown hair was really Axiom-man. Erring on the side of caution came first and he thought maybe the idea of retiring the geeky Gabriel Garrison persona was premature. Right now, he needed to keep Gabriel and Axiom-man as far away from each other as possible and having identities on opposite sides of the personality spectrum seemed a good way to do that.

*This sucks, man. Now I got to keep acting like a wimp,* he thought.

There was a soft knock at his door and his heart leaped in his chest. He froze, held his breathe, and hoped whoever it was would move on. A minute later, the knock came again. Gabriel *shifted* and floated off the floor thus eliminating the sound of his approach. At the door, he peered through the peephole and a jolt shot through him when he saw Valerie standing on the other side.

*What's she doing here?* Not that he wasn't grateful to see her, but for her to just show up out of the blue like this really caught him off guard. *She no doubt knows what's happening out there. Maybe she thinks I'm innocent otherwise why else would she be here?*

He didn't know if he should open the door though. Hand poised above the knob, he made a fist to stop his trembling fingers.

*What if she has the police with her? She knows who I am.* He wasn't in the mood for another firefight. He waited. She stayed there.

She knocked again, then his cellphone rang in the living room. He peeked through the peephole and saw her with her phone to her ear. She leaned in close to the door at the same time as if listening for something. Quickly, he hovered over to his phone and shut the ringer off.

She texted him: *i know ur there. heard ur phone.*

He shook his head.

She wrote again: *pls lemme in. im alone.*

After a pause: *pls?*

He hovered back to the door and gently touched down. After *shifting* his powers off, he took a deep breath and put his hand on the knob, the other hand poised by the security chain.

*Be ready for anything.* He was set to *shift* at a moment's notice.

He undid the chain, the deadbolt and the knob lock, and opened the door.

All she said was a gentle, "Hi."

———

Oscar Owen stood before the vault in his office. It was new, his Redsaw suit now within. He hadn't put it on since the night the Doorway opened, but the time to do so was fast approaching. Try as he might to step away from what was laid before him, the dark power within him compelled him to imagine and dream what giving into it would entail. The way the master spoke of his destiny implied he didn't have a choice in the matter. He was never one to "not have a choice," but, it seemed, the power within was dictating his actions, even if just subtly. And the draw to the suit, to use it to help facilitate his master's arrival on Earth was nearly overwhelming.

He wouldn't be able to hold out much longer.

Time was running out.

————

Gabriel was still stunned Valerie was here. She simply sat on his couch in his living room, looking at him; he was at a loss for what to say. He sat on the chair by his computer, his eyes to the floor.

He couldn't raise his face to see her. He wanted to ask her how she was, if she had healed up okay after the kidnapping, but instead remained quiet, suddenly ashamed he couldn't have gotten to her sooner. He'd had no way of knowing she'd been taken when the city had been covered in Bleaken's black cloud, but he still felt responsible.

"I'm alone in case you're worried," she said.

He kept his eyes to the floor. "To be honest, I wasn't sure. I'm sorry."

"Don't be."

He looked up. Her brown hair had gotten longer, and seemingly gotten darker, too, though that could've been his imagination. Her brown eyes carried a sense of warmth and she seemed somehow different than before. "How are you?"

"Overall, pretty good. I'm healing okay, but I have nightmares still. My counselor says they should go away in time as long as I don't keep dwelling on them."

"I'm sorry for not getting there sooner, Val."

It was a small smile, but it broke the ice. "You came when you found out."

*I'd do anything for you.* "I'm sorry for not telling you sooner. I was going to, but couldn't bring myself to doing it."

"It needed to happen on its own, though I admit I was hoping things would've panned out differently. Guess I was the one who ended up speaking first."

"How did you know? Did you recognize me?"

She shook her head and blushed. "That night at the Fort Garry Hotel. Our dance. You held me a certain way. That's when I knew because Axiom-man held me the same way. Your hands seemed to find the same place both times, the same touch, the same care. It just seemed to . . . fit."

He couldn't help but smile a little himself. "I feel like I lied to you."

"It's not lying. It's just not telling . . . everything."

"Yeah, but the way I was around you—that guy, the glasses, the screwups—that's not me. It's all an act."

"Take the fun out of it, why don't ya?" she said with a smirk.

"What?"

"Kidding. It was a bit transparent at times, now that I think about it. But it was kind of cute in a weird way."

He was so happy she was being so open and taking it all so remarkably well. For the first time ever in their relationship it seemed they could be completely real with each other. No secrets. No games.

The mood suddenly sobered. "It's not me," he said.

"What?"

"It's not me, out there, doing those things. I swear to you it's somebody else."

"I know. I thought—at first, mind you—I thought maybe you finally buckled under the strain of doing what you do, that somehow you just had enough, got angry and, with your power, just, well . . . just went crazy, to be blunt. I know after the close calls I experienced, it started to take its toll on me and I felt things breaking inside." She finally took off her jacket. "It would've made sense, in a way, you losing it. I don't know how you cope."

*Because I have to.* He didn't want to get into it and tell her there was more at stake than even someone masquerading as him going around causing death and destruction. The upcoming inevitable battle with Redsaw—whenever that was—was about more than just power or control. He shoved the thoughts away. "The police didn't contact you, did they?"

"Why?"

"Because of your affiliation with me."

She looked at him quizzically.

"With Axiom-man. He—I—rescued you a few times and I thought maybe they'd talk to you to see if you knew anything. I mean, I showed up in my gear at the hospital after you got hurt, after all."

"No. Not even a phone call. Speaking of which, I was going to call earlier, but wasn't sure what I'd say or how to even say it. I thought coming here might . . . might lay all the cards on the table. I'm sorry for kicking you out of my hospital room."

"It's my fault. You'd been through so much and the last thing you needed was some emotional avalanche from me."

She gave a slow nod. "Do you have any idea who this guy is?"

"No. I thought it was Redsaw, but the guy had gone dark a while ago and, you see, he and I have this kind of weird thing where I can sense his presence if my powers are turned on." *Granted, I haven't been around this other Axiom-man so don't know for sure.*

"Turned on?"

He stood from the chair and thought a little display might lighten the mood. He knew he sure needed it and she probably did, too. "Ready?"

"For?"

He *shifted* and knew she saw his hair take on a blue hue and his eyes light up with sparkling bright blue energy. He wondered if she even noticed the new aura that covered his skin.

"Cool," she said slowly. "So that's how it works. I thought you were wearing a wig or something."

He ran his hand through his hair. "Why? Does it look like a wig?"

"No, I mean, later, when I thought about it, I wondered how the whole hair color change thing went. Thought maybe a wig was part of your costume." Her irises looked to the side then met his. "Can I see it?"

"The suit?"

She nodded, eyes lit up.

"Okay, I guess." He didn't know why at first, but then thought that from her perspective this all must be pretty awesome. He went to his bedroom, retrieved his gear, then came back with it in his arms. It wasn't put together as the dark blue bodysuit was separate from the light blue chest piece and cape. He let the dark blue part hang down in front of him then held the cape and chest piece partly in front of it. He held the mask and gloves in the other hand.

Valerie sat there and looked at it like she was star-struck. She stood, came over, and slowly put her palm on his uniform. When she looked at him, she studied his glowing eyes. Smiling, she turned away as if catching herself gushing.

Gabriel tossed his costume over his chair, *shifted* his powers down, and came up behind her, gently putting his hands on her shoulders. She was warm and smelled so good. When she didn't pull away, he wrapped his arms all the way around her. She turned within his embrace and hugged him, laying her head against his shoulder.

He held her tight. After the past few days of being the object of everyone's hate, it felt so good to be wanted again.

It felt so good to be with Valerie again after all this time apart.

# CHAPTER ELEVEN

VALERIE HAD WANTED to go flying, but Gabriel said they couldn't, not with the police looking for him. Even if he wore another fake costume, he couldn't run the risk of Valerie accidentally getting hurt if he had to touch down somewhere and help someone, or because he spotted the imposter. She was disappointed, he knew, and so was he, but it was for the best.

Instead, they held hands and walked Corydon Avenue, the city's popular strip with restaurants, coffee shops, a candy store, and a couple of clubs.

"Hungry?" he asked. He pushed his glasses up higher on his nose. After that guy had knocked them off, they kept slipping and he didn't have a small enough screwdriver to tighten the arm. Valerie didn't even ask about the faint red line still on his face from it.

"Not really. A bit overwhelmed."

"Why? You didn't picture our first date as walking around here?"

"Is that what this is? A date?"

Good question. It was more than just them walking around, now that he thought about it. "No, you're right. This is more casual than I had hoped, but we did have that date at the Fort Garry Hotel, remember?"

She chuckled. "Yeah, but that wasn't really real now, was it? You were putting on a show the entire time."

"And you didn't know." He smiled.

"There were times when I thought it was a bit too much, like I said, but there were also times when I thought that's how you really were and if I was going to be friends with you, I'd better get used to it."

"Well, I hope you're happy going forward."

She gave him a confused look.

"I meant, I hope . . . and I don't want to sound stupid . . . but I hope you like me for me. The real me. No show. No act."

She smiled. "I'm sure I will."

As amazing as it was to be spending time with her again, Gabriel's mind kept wandering to the idea that somewhere out there was a dangerous super-powered villain planning his next attack, if not already in the middle of it. He had told Valerie before they left this would be a short jaunt because he had Axiom-man work to do, and the only reason he didn't just tell her to hold off and they'd hang out another time was because he knew he needed to be with her to refresh himself, put closure on the bumps in their past, and just enjoy her company and clear his head so he could face whatever was next.

They passed by a coffee place and went in.

"Coffee for me," Gabriel said, patting his pants for his wallet. He was light on the dough but this was Valerie he was with.

"This late?" she asked. "Oh, right."

"You?"

"Tea. Earl Grey."

"Hot," he said.

"What? How's that h—"

"Sorry. *Star Trek* thing."

"You're a Trekkie?"

"Trekk*er*," he corrected.

"Oh my. Won't we have a lot to talk about."

*Are you serious? She's into* Star Trek*! How cool is that?* It was their turn to order so Gabriel did for both of them. He paid for both, too, and they chose a quiet table in the corner after they dressed their drinks at the station off to the side.

When they sat down, he asked, "You talking the new movies or TV stuff?"

"For *Star Trek*?"

He nodded.

"Both. The new flicks rock pretty hard, though. It's like they merged *Star Wars* and *Star Trek* together."

"Best of both worlds," he said with a smirk.

"Great episode, by the way."

"You caught that one, huh?" *Best of both Worlds* was one of his favorite *Star Trek: The Next Generation* two-parters. Being a sucker for time travel, *Time's Arrow* was also pretty cool.

"As much as I enjoy the new ones, I think my favorite Trek flick is *First Contact*," she said.

"Mine, too. *TNG*'s my favorite."

"Mine, too."

"Okay, that's enough," he said playfully. He was grinning like an idiot. He couldn't help it and didn't care. He took a sip of his coffee. She had some of her tea.

"I liked *Voyager*, too, but it didn't hook me the same as *TNG*. Some good episodes, though."

"I feel the same way."

"Stop it, Gabriel."

"No, really. I'm glad they used a ship again after the 'stationary' episodes of *DS9*. Those had some good ones, too, by the way—and I liked the *Defiant*—but *Voyager* didn't have the same depth as *TNG*. Could've been the characters. They were interesting, but didn't seem as real as Picard and Riker and all them."

Lip of her tea cup in her mouth, she could only nod.

They talked for a long while about *Star Trek*, *Star Wars* and even superheroes, though he could tell Valerie seemed unsure if speaking about that last one was okay in public or not. He knew she was only trying not to draw attention to their conversation. Maybe she was afraid she'd accidentally say something that would give him away? A few times he caught her just sitting there, staring at him, a look on her face saying, "I know who you really are." He was sure she had a million questions, but those would have to wait.

He checked his watch. It was getting late and they had stayed out longer than he meant to. As they walked back to his apartment, they held hands again.

"How'd you get to my place?" he asked.

"Bus."

"I'd really like you to take a cab home," he said. "I'll pay for it." *Not that I can afford it.* But her safety came first. "It'll be faster and it's not a public service in the way the buses are. I'm worried something might happen."

"I had the news on before I came. There's another curfew going into effect starting tomorrow night."

"I heard."

"Police said this one will be strictly enforced, no compromise. Anyone caught out will be fined and, depending on where they're caught and what they're doing, could face some jail time."

"I don't think they could throw you in the clink for that long just for breaking curfew."

"Not years, obviously, but a few days until you learned your lesson, I'm sure. What do you think of it?"

"The curfew?"

"More so the idea that one guy seems to have the whole city under his thumb because he's causing trouble."

"He needs to be stopped and it needs to be now. Valerie, you don't understand how" —his voice went quiet and not for the need of secrecy; the sudden ache in his heart brought it down— "it's so hard knowing people are out there dying because of me."

"You're not doing this."

"Not me, but *because* of me. There's lots you don't know, but when I first got my powers, it started something really big and really important."

"Such as?"

He sighed. "I can't tell you. Not yet. Now's not the time. It's too late and I have work to do, and it's a big conversation."

"Is it scary?"

He wasn't going to lie to her. He was through doing that. "Yeah, pretty scary, but not if I do my job, which is why it's so important I catch this guy. My presence in this city started this whole thing and it got worse after that night at the MTS Centre."

"When you fought Redsaw," she said quietly. Then, "What happened?"

"It's a long, long story, but know that I'll figure this out."

"I want you to know that you're doing a good job. This city is safer because of you. What's happening with this other guy pretending to be you aside, you've made a huge difference and saved this city more than once. People talk. Before, many weren't sure what to make of you, but they're on your side now." She seemed to have caught herself. "I mean—"

"I know what you mean. I hope that I can win them back once this guy is captured."

"You will, and it'll be quick once the truth comes out."

They walked in silence for a few moments, Gabriel keeping his eyes open for a cab. He'd flag it down the moment he saw one. "We spent a lot of time talking about me. What about you?"

"You mean we spent a lot of time talking about *Star Trek*."

"You know what I mean."

"What about me?"

"How's work?"

"Busy. We moved offices. I don't know if you know that."

"I guessed as much once the tower was finished. You still doing the same thing or . . . ?"

"Kinda. New position, but a lot of the same tasks or variations of them. Executive Assistant is my official title. Answer to Mr. Owen directly and he's got me doing so much that sometimes it feels like I'm co-running the place though I know that's an exaggeration."

"What's he do, again? Real estate?"

"A bit of everything, it seems. Started out doing those payday loan places, made a bunch of money, then got into real estate. Writes eBooks, too, apparently, the how-to kind. Always has one on the go. Says it's where he got his start and so does it out of tradition and for the money, of course. Now he's got some other stuff going on that I'm not allowed to talk about. He's built quite the empire in a real short time, but he's also dealing with huge numbers regularly so I suppose when you got big transactions coming in and going out of your business all the time, you can grow rapidly."

"Sounds . . . cool." He meant to say, "interesting." He was tempted to ask her to put in a good word for him for a job, but didn't know how to bring it up. Gabriel didn't want to say he recently found himself suddenly out of work. It was embarrassing. Here he was, a superhero on the one hand and an out-of-work guy in his mid-twenties with no qualifications on the other.

"What about you? What's going on at Dolla-card these days?"

"Well . . . not much. You see—" A cab came into view up ahead. "Hold on." *Saved by the cab.* Gabriel stepped close to the curb and raised his hand, giving the cab a wave. He dug out his wallet and pulled out a couple of twenties. He gave them to Valerie. "Take this."

She lifted her purse. "Gabriel, I got it. I got a good job."

"I insist."

She folded the bills back into his hand. "And I insist you keep it. I'm a big girl. I can pay for my own cab."

"But—"

"Enough." She gave him that look that said she was serious: eyes slightly wide, staring straight into his, lips pressed together.

"Okay. Thanks."

The cab pulled up. She took his hands, leaned in close and gave him a kiss on the cheek. "Be careful, okay?"

"Call me when you get home?"

"Deal."

"We'll do this right when things settle down, okay?"

"You better."

Their eyes locked and he so desperately wanted to kiss her. It seemed like she wanted him to as well, but he wasn't going to, not with the cab waiting. He'd rather it be something they could take their time with instead of rushing it along. She smiled, then gave his hands a squeeze. He returned the affection; she let go and got into the cab.

After the door closed, he gave her the Vulcan sign for "Live long and prosper."

She burst out laughing behind the window as the cab drove away.

# Chapter Twelve

GABRIEL HAD TAKEN an old black T-shirt, cut a couple of eye holes in it, then wrapped it around his head in a makeshift, full-faced mask. For the rest of his crude ensemble, he opted for a simple black sweatsuit, figuring all the black would help him blend into the shadows better and also help hide him against the night sky if anyone was looking up. He used the same gloves as the last outfit. Same with the shoes.

Feeling energized after his evening with Valerie, he swooped over the city, once again hoping against hope he'd find the fake Axiom-man.

As he flew, he was careful to maintain a fairly high altitude to blend against the night sky. He hoped it wouldn't be to his detriment as by doing so he couldn't see the finer points of what was going on below.

He was loving this new flight speed, however. He'd kick it into high gear every so often and test maneuvering at such high velocity. It'd take some getting used to as physics didn't totally abandon him, and with greater speed came more momentum so sharply cutting to the left or right took a tremendous amount of even his ultra strength to pull off.

Up ahead, sirens blared loud and clear. There must've been six or seven of them sounding all at once. He flew closer and, looking at the street far below, saw several squad cars, two fire trucks and a couple of ambulances all heading down Broadway. Other cars pulled out of their way to let them pass.

*This is it,* he thought. *Something's happened and they're off to hopefully catch him.* "That means I got to get there, too."

He kept up with the emergency vehicles below no problem, the flashing emergency lights acting as a beacon and allowing him to maintain his altitude and keep himself out of sight as much as possible. He wouldn't make his presence known unless needed. First, he had to know exactly what was going on.

The emergency vehicles pulled up in front of an apartment building. Axiom-man slowed his flight and hovered in the air high above and across from the scene. Upon further assessment, and as he watched the cops pour from their vehicles, all the emergency workers looked up toward the top of the building. Axiom-man followed their line of sight and saw a man in a green T-shirt holding a woman against himself, standing at the edge of the building's roof. The guy was shouting something, but he was too far away to make it out. He slowly floated closer so he could hear.

"She's dead meat! I'm serious. Don't send anyone up or I throw her off!" The guy held something in his hand and held it against the woman's jaw. Axiom-man couldn't tell if it was a knife or a gun.

Below, some of the cops were at the front door to the apartment building, trying to buzz their way in. A couple others rounded the building to either side, presumably to see if there was a fire escape or some other means to climb up. The building was six stories so wasn't terribly high, but if the man pushed that woman off, she'd be done for.

*Need to take him out from a distance, if I can help it,* Axiom-man thought. He considered zapping the man just enough to send him reeling back but without killing him, but if he did that, there was a chance he'd let loose with whatever was in his hand and the woman would get hurt.

A cut to the face was one thing, but if he slashed her jugular or, if it was a gun, shot her, she wouldn't make it.

With his new flight speed, he could get in their quickly and get out just as quick, too.

Below, EMTs readied a gurney. The firefighters were getting set up.

"Going to kill her, man, I swear!" the guy yelled.

The woman wailed.

"Shut up!"

*Get in, get out,* Axiom-man told himself. He flew over to the other side of the building so he'd come in high and from the rear. "Here we go," he whispered, and kicked on the speed. He flew in hard and quick, an immediate rush of cool air blowing against him. When he was about fifteen or twenty feet from the guy, he abruptly put on the brakes and skidded to a halt on the roof. The sound of his feet landing was louder than he expected. He had wanted to do it more gracefully and land unannounced then storm the guy, tear him off her before he could react, and put him down.

The man spun around, girl in hand. He shouted over his shoulder. "I said, don't send anyone up!"

The woman's face was glistening with tears. "Please, please help me."

Axiom-man raised his hands. "We can work this out." He saw the weapon. It *was* a gun. "Put it down and let's talk."

"No talking. I ain't going back inside, man."

It took a second to register what he meant. He was talking about jail. What did he do that got this whole thing going? "We can try to avoid that if you co-operate." That totally wasn't true, but he did say "try."

"Never! Never again."

Axiom-man attempted to take a step closer, but the guy gave the girl a jerk and pulled her tighter to himself. The two remained at the edge of the building.

"Please," Axiom-man said, "let her go."

The man waited before responding and looked to somewhere past him.

*Good. He's considering it. That was eas—* A jolt of electricity shot through him, its tingle sharp and deep, causing his muscles to lock. Yet he was still able to move . . . slowly. He turned around and saw a cord running from his back to a wide-eyed cop's Taser. There were two policemen on the roof with four more coming up through the roof access hatch.

*A setup. Again.* Axiom-man's arm felt as slow as molasses as he moved to pull the cord. He gave it a yank and the deep vibrations from the electrical discharge ceased a second later. He had expected to feel the pinch of the prongs dislodging from his skin even through his clothes, but felt nothing. The cop reached for his gun.

Axiom-man leaned to the right and put on his flight.

Gunshots followed.

As Axiom-man zipped along the roof to the apartment next door, debris shot up around him as the bullets pierced the roofing. He quickly dipped down over the edge of the building, flying face first toward the parking lot on the other side. He slowed his flight as best he could, the sudden stop sending his body flipping forward, landing him on his back on the cement. Every muscle and bone lit up with pain from the impact and the sudden jolt forced him to lay still for a moment. His muscles still tingled from getting hit with the Taser, but it hadn't fully paralyzed him. He didn't know why, then thought maybe the recent surge and his new aura had something to do with it. No time to dwell on that now, however.

Rushing footsteps.

Cops.

He rolled over onto his side and started to float off the ground, quickly ascending higher until he was clear of the roofs and rising into the sky.

Gunshots went off below and bullets whizzed past him.

*Where are they shooting from?* He looked back at the scene and didn't see anyone. More gunshots went off, these in rapid succession. Bullets zipped past him and one cut straight through the side of his hand. He snapped it to his chest with a yelp. It stung like crazy and the flesh surrounding the wound burned hot and deep. He couldn't bend his fingers either. He hoped the tendons hadn't been severed and it was just a flesh wound.

More gunshots rang out even as he flew further downtown. He was far enough away from the apartment building so there was no way anyone was shooting at him from there.

He scanned the buildings below and saw that every other rooftop had someone on them standing next to a mounted rifle on a tripod.

Shots rang out as he flew overhead.

"Screw this," he said and arced upward, getting as high into the sky as he could. Shots still followed and he assumed the scopes on the weapons were fairly powerful therefore he needed some major distance before he had a chance to truly get away.

Fire lit up his leg as a bullet tore through his calf. Screaming from the impact, he instinctively slowed his flight as he reached for his leg, then when he caught himself doing so he poured on the speed again. Height and distance was everything at the moment.

All he could think was: *I'm shot, I'm shot, I'm shot . . .*

And there was no one he could turn to without getting turned in himself.

------

After coming home, Valerie had called Gabriel to let him know she was okay, then had a hot bath to wind down and relax before bed. Now she lay there, unable to sleep, her mind spinning with memories of her evening, wondering if Gabriel would call her tomorrow, how she could see him between her late hours and the curfew starting tomorrow night, and what Gabriel was going to do about the madman on the loose. Never mind she had a million and one things to do for the office and with the grand opening ceremony in a few days, Mr. Owen wanted her at work early Monday morning to finalize the outdoor set up for the ribbon cutting ceremony, the hors d'oeuvres and cocktail party in the lobby after, not to mention making sure teardown went smoothly as well. She also had to field media inquiries, arrange arrivals and departures for some, and ensure security was doubled for the event.

"Must. Go. To. Sleep," she told herself. *The more you try, the worse it is.* She had hoped the hot bath would've knocked her out. It was one of her reasons for taking it. She didn't have any sleeping pills and she wasn't about to load up on cold medication simply because she knew it'd make her drowsy.

She thought back to her outing with Gabriel. When she had gone to his apartment tonight, she hadn't expected them to go out for coffee. She simply wanted to clear the air between them and let him know she was there for him and that she didn't believe he was the one killing people. As they talked, she finally got to spend time with the real him. She saw glimpses of the Gabriel she worked with, the goofy smiles, the politeness and courtesies—like him carrying her tea to the table for her—and she saw bits of Axiom-man, too: the occasional dip in his voice, confidence, quiet strength and a genuine distaste for the mayhem the city was currently undergoing. Even the way he carried himself fluctuated between a slouch and standing with his shoulders back while he found his footing with her.

The more time went on, the more she felt these little connections happen, as if she was syncing up with him piece by piece. She never thought she'd feel so at ease with anyone and admire someone so much at the same time. She was also intimidated a little, too. Gabriel was something bigger than life, someone who dealt with things that even the most noble peacemakers never did. And his powers . . . she wondered what it'd be like to be able to fly, to be stronger than everyone else, to have this crackling energy emit from her eyes and shine over her body.

She wondered if she would've made the same choice as him and used those abilities to help others instead of helping herself. Shamefully, she admitted that at one point she might've used them for selfish gain, but since Axiom-man appeared—*Gabriel*—and seeing the potential of using such power for good . . . she knew that if the opportunity ever presented itself for her to join him that she would do the same. She wasn't sure about the costume part, at least, one that was skin-tight, but that remained to be seen.

Her phone rang on her dresser.

"Who's calling at one in the morning?" She got out of bed and checked the number. It was the front door, the callbox synced up so she could buzz people in. It was a new feature for her apartment building. She answered. "Hello?"

"Val? It's me. I . . . I need your help."

*Gabriel.*

# CHAPTER THIRTEEN

When Valerie opened the door, Gabriel, clad in all black, hair slicked with sweat, stumbled in and collapsed on her landing mat.

"Close the door," he said quietly.

She did and saw the pant leg of his sweatpants. The fabric looked burned. Same with one of his gloves.

"What happened?" she asked.

He rolled onto his back and forced himself to sit up. "I'm sorry." He winced. "I . . . I cauterized it as best I could, but I think I made it worse."

"Did you—"

"Police. Guns. Bullets."

She put a hand to her mouth and tears immediately welled in her eyes. She didn't realize she'd be so concerned so quickly. Though she knew better, a part of her considered Axiom-man invincible.

She had to look away from all the dry and crusted blood. "You need to go to a hospital."

"Can't. Cops'll investigate any gunshot wounds."

"Gunshot?"

He nodded. "I needed to take care of it myself. I only came here because your place was closer than mine. What I assume is the Special Force Unit have snipers on the majority of the city rooftops. Probably a combination of them and the military. Couldn't even fly here but had to walk. Was able to float for part of it, stick to the shadows, but as the streetlights got more frequent, I had to lose the mask unless someone saw me all in black sneaking around." He pulled what looked like a T-shirt with eye holes cut into it out of the band of his sweatpants.

"Tried to play it casual. Hard to do when you're limping like crazy."

"I don't know what to do."

"Keep the lights down." He glanced over his shoulder and further into her apartment. "Bathroom."

"Let me help you up." She reached down and helped him to his feet. He wasn't a big guy, but was pretty heavy. Either that or she wasn't as strong as she thought she was. With one arm around her shoulder, she helped him hop into the bathroom. Once he was in, she left him for a second to shut off her bedroom light and the one in the hallway. She supposed that if by chance someone had followed him here, they'd look for the apartment with a light on, and in the middle of the night, hers would be one of maybe three. At least in the block she lived in. The bathroom didn't have a window so the light could stay on in there.

When she returned, Gabriel sat at the edge of the tub, his leg drawn up, wincing as he examined the burnt fabric that seemed glued to his leg.

"I don't know if it went all the way through. I hope so because I'd have no idea how to fish it out and I'd probably make myself bleed to death even if I tied it off."

"What can I get you?"

"I've only done a bit of research into this kind of thing. Part of equipping myself should it ever happen and, well . . . . Anyway, I need scissors, a cloth—a few of them, actually—a bowl of water, tweezers, needle and thread, and some major painkillers."

"I got T3s."

"Really?"

"Wisdom tooth operation. Long time ago. Never finished the bottle but kept them on hand for the occasional vicious headache. Haven't used them in over a year though so don't know if they're still good."

"Should be fine. Something's better than nothing. I don't know about that stuff anyway. Got any booze? Hard stuff like whiskey or rum?"

"You're not mixing painkillers and alcohol."

"For the wound, unless you have rubbing alcohol."

"Might have some peroxide. You're not putting booze on that. Come on, think straight."

"Right. Sorry."

She stared at the wound and her stomach turned. "Sorry. I'm sidetracked. What do you need again?"

He rattled off the list to her once more and wiped the sweat off his brow. He was clearly in a lot of pain, but was doing a pretty good job of stuffing it down. Valerie went off and brought him what he needed in three trips.

When she brought the last of it, he was examining his hand. A chunk of flesh was missing from the side of his palm about an inch beneath his pinky, the flesh there burnt as well. She gave him a couple of T3s and a glass of water.

"Thanks," he said as he took it with his good hand. He shoved the pills in his mouth and chugged down the water. "Can I have some more? Real thirsty."

"Sure." She refilled the glass at the sink then gave it to him. He drank it down just as greedily then handed the glass back to her.

"I'm going to need your help. This hand is numb and I can barely move it. I don't think anything's broken, but this is a two-handed thing."

She sat down on the toilet, which was next to the tub. *Just be strong, girl.* She looked at the pant leg and the gummy-looking seared fabric that was attached to his skin. The smell was awful, a cross between burnt hair and charred meat.

"It's gross, I know, sorry," he said. His eyes met hers. With a smile, he said, "What a night, huh?"

She couldn't help but smile back. "You're telling me."

He handed her the scissors. "Here, help me cut all the excess material off, then I'm going to tie off the wound and remove what parts of the material I burned to myself. Hopefully I can sew it shut."

"It's going to get infected."

"We'll wash it with the peroxide."

"You have any idea how much that's going to sting?"

"I don't have a choice, Val."

"I hope you know what you're doing."

"Not really. Just need to take our time and . . ." He didn't finish. "Can you just start cutting?" He cleared his throat. "Sorry. I don't mean to snap. It just hurts so much."

Steeling herself against the awful sight of burnt flesh covered in dried blood and crusty material, she started to remove the excess fabric.

———

It was nearly an hour later by the time they were done cutting away the rest of the pant leg along with meticulously stripping the wound of the burnt fabric. The T3s had helped with the pain and constant dabbing at the wound with a peroxide-soaked cloth helped clean the blood that started to leak. It stung like crazy, though, and each time Gabriel had to wait a few moments for the wave of burning agony to settle down before he and Valerie started picking at the scabbing again. He needed to find the entry hole, which he figured was on the side.

The exit wound was through the back. Between the burnt skin and scabbing, it was hard to find the proper point and he didn't want to just go tearing up his leg. His foot and leg from just above the knee down was stark white from the circulation having been cut off.

"I think that's it," he said as he peeled away a layer of scab.

Valerie turned away. "Ewww . . ."

"Sorry." When the scabbing was removed, blood immediately started to pump out. His heart raced into a panic as it gushed out of his leg, onto the floor, onto Valerie and himself. Did the tourniquet come loose? He checked. It was still in place. Something had gone horribly wrong.

With wide-eyes, he said, "Call an ambulance. Tell them you saw a guy collapsed in the middle of the road out back. Block your number. Call it in after I leave and stay here."

"You'll leave a trail."

"Not if I go out through the balcony. I'm going to fly down."

"You'll be arrested."

"But you'll be safe. Please. Call it in. I'm sorry about the mess." He *shifted* and powered up. With a growl from the pain, he zapped the wound with his eye beams and Valerie yelped as the flesh popped and sizzled. Using his flight, he floated to his feet and told her to get to her phone.

Wanting as much distance from her as fast as possible for her own good, he quickly went through her living room and out the balcony, where he flew down to street level and stood in the middle of the road. A few agonizing minutes later, sirens rose on the air. He *shifted* his powers off and lay down on the road. He tore the wound open and swallowed the pain. The paramedics would seal his leg and an investigation would be underway as to who this "John Doe" was. Not wanting his face to be on record, but also knowing he couldn't wear his mask—which he left up in Valerie's place anyway—he rolled his eyes when he realized what he had to do.

*It worked before.* Gabriel balled up his fist and broke his nose and gave himself a black eye.

The T3s didn't help the pain for that, but he was happy the swelling would disguise him, and in turn, would help keep Valerie safe.

# Chapter Fourteen

It was the final day of preparation for the Owen Tower grand opening and Valerie was back at the office fielding calls left, right and center to get things done. To make things worse, a few folks had called in sick so there was no one to pass some of the tasks on to to help ease the pressure. But her duties at her job were the least of her worries. Gabriel was constantly on her mind, and more than once since he left her apartment she was tempted to start calling around the hospitals to see if someone matching his description was there so she could find out how he was.

If he was okay, that was.

No news of Axiom-man's arrest had hit the media so maybe Gabriel had stayed one step ahead of the cops after all?

She couldn't see him, though, lest she run the risk of giving away who he really was. If only Gabriel had a doctor or even a nurse who would help him "off the record" when things like this happened. He should also seriously look at bulletproofing his costume going forward, and she made a mental note to bring up these concerns the next time she saw him. Maybe that would be her role once all this settled? Being a behind-the-scenes guide or assistant to Axiom-man as well being Gabriel's . . . well, there wasn't an official title for that yet. Hopefully girlfriend, but nothing was set in stone.

As hurt as Gabriel was, what was even more disturbing was that the city was now left unprotected and the longer Gabriel spent in the hospital, the longer the Axiom-man imposter would be on the loose. And the more lives would be lost to his senseless violence. She only hoped that if the imposter attacked again, that whatever he did wouldn't be catastrophic and any casualties would be kept to a minimum. It seemed unlikely, though, as each attack seemed to increase with severity and loss of life.

Her phone rang and the call display read it was from the mayor's office. Taking a quick moment to clear her mind, Valerie inhaled a deep breath, exhaled slowly, then picked up the phone.

———

Swimming the lanes was the only form of relaxation Glen found these days, and after the knee replacements, powerlifting was no longer an option. It sucked, too, because he had been a major player on the Strongman circuits and was poised to take the nationals next year, but after years of heavy training, even the strongest joints sometimes gave out. He was only forty-two and thought he had many years of competing left and always supposed major injuries were for the older guys. The *really* older guys. After being laid up for four months after surgery and going through rehab, he tried hitting the gym only to find he had lost a lot of power, his knees hurting every time he put some strain on them. On doctor's orders, he was to take a year off and only do light exercise. Swimming was recommended. Turned out he really enjoyed it and made it an afternoon ritual to hit the lanes and squeeze off as many laps in an hour as he could.

There were three pools in Elmwood Kildonan Pool. A shallow one on the end for children and families, one in the middle of medium depth for doing laps, and the third at the far end the deepest for diving. All three were packed, especially with young people. Must've been an inservice today.

On lap thirty-three, Glen was feeling pretty good. As he reached into the water, he tilted his head to the side, eyes closed, mouth open, getting a lungful of air before getting ready to put his face down and blow out as he brought his other arm around. Ear in the water, he suddenly stopped his swim when a loud *GALOOMP* sounded beneath the surface. He righted himself, treading. Waves rolled up around him. Everyone else in the lanes had stopped, too. He scanned the water and saw a giant dark shape rising from the bottom of the pool. It shot through the surface with a splash. He pulled off his goggles to get a better look. He recognized the shape as part of the ceiling's wooden beams and the heavy metal bracket that joined them.

"Everybody out!" the lifeguard shouted, blowing his whistle.

The whole place started to panic, people screaming and rushing toward the sides of the pool and to the change rooms. Before anyone could reach the doors leading out, the ceiling above that area came crashing down, sending them jumping back almost to the pool's edge. They tried running the perimeter of the pools to get to the emergency exits on the other side, but the roof came plummeting down there as well, sending out large chunks of wood, metal, and dust.

Some people lost their balance on the edge of the pool and fell in.

Glen looked up, trying to see what caused the collapse, but only saw the blue sky beyond.

More sections of the ceiling began to come down, sending people to the bulkheads that divided the pools. Some made it on, others were shoved to the side, falling into the water. A couple cracked their heads on the edge of the pool before going in; blood fogged up the water.

People shoved past Glen to try and get to the edges and climb out. His size and weight, even in the water, helped keep him afloat as they pushed past. Across the way, a young man was desperately trying to climb out, but others clawed past him, shoving him down beneath the surface. He bobbed up, gasping for air, only to be plunged back down again. Glen swam over; he took an elbow to the face as someone flailed their arms as they swam past him. He wiped the blood leaking from his nose and went straight for the young man, who had just been sent below the surface for at least the fourth time. Glen got his arm around his chest, pulled his head above water, and started swimming backward.

The guy gasped and sputtered, clearly panicking.

"It's okay, I got you," Glen said, adjusting his body so it was underneath the young man's, helping the guy keep his head and chest above water.

The guy coughed again and managed a weak, "Thanks."

More chunks of the ceiling came down. Glen looked up and the surviving band of ceiling that ran over the place like a wooden and metallic rainbow began to shake, its rumble sending vibrations into the walls and into the pool. Axiom-man flew between the gaps in the ceiling, bringing his fists down on the remaining roofing, sending chunks of it crashing down into the water below. Some of the debris hit people, cracking their heads. Other pieces tagged folks in the shoulders. More ceiling fell down along the sides, sending everyone into the pool where they waved their arms, kicking and splashing in sheer pandemonium.

Huge waves erupted from the chaos and Glen fought to keep the young man's head above the surface. The guy was still disoriented so he must've taken in a lot of water before Glen rescued him. He pulled on him and took him to the center of the pool where it was a bit calmer thanks to everyone else streaming for the sides, trying to climb out. Obstacles of roof debris made getting out impossible now.

More of the ceiling came crashing down from above and Glen's world slowed when he saw a huge jagged piece of wood come spiking for his head. He tried to turn away but took it hard at the crown of his skull, the force of it sending him under. The water around him instantly turned warm and he knew his head had been split open. He tried to surface, but the young man he held suddenly felt heavier.

*Come on, push!* Glen thought and forced the young man up. He was able to get a gulp of air himself before dizziness stole his worldview and fogginess crept around the edges of his vision. His world tipped backward and he sunk below the water's surface. As he went down, he saw more ceiling coming down from beneath the surface.

He got his head up somehow and had to right the young man, who had gone face down in the water. Glen got under him and held him, his body growing weaker from the loss of blood. As the rest of the ceiling came down, he slowly sunk below the surface and swore he'd keep the young man up above the water as long as he could hold out.

---

Gabriel blinked open his eyes, the hospital room blurry, but slowly coming back into focus. He was hooked up to an I.V. and he was pain-free but groggy. As the world returned into view and his brain went back online, he figured they must have him hooked up to a pretty solid painkiller at the moment. He shuffled underneath his covers and through swollen eyes saw his leg wrapped in bandage and gauze from the knee down. He looked at his hand and it was wrapped, too. His other hand . . . the faint blue glow was gone. His powers must've shut off while he was under. Touching his face, checking for the swelling, he was relieved to find he was bandaged.

Someone sat in a chair across from the bed and his heart sank when he saw who it was: Jack Gunn. The man stared straight at him. Even had his weapon drawn.

"Don't try anything," Jack said. The guy still wore that trench coat of his, even indoors, like a second skin. He raised the gun as if to show he meant business.

"You don't need that."

"The heck I don't. Not after you've escaped me before. I need to be ready for anything."

*How'd he find me?* Then he realized Jack must've had all hospitals on alert and to report any gunshot wounds or suspicious persons. *So much for my idea of keeping them out of this.* Yet he knew the risk when getting Valerie to phone it in. He hoped she had taken his advice and blocked her number.

"I guess we're finding out how human you really are, huh?" Jack said. "Maybe you're not so *super* after all."

"What do you want?"

Jack sighed. "Looks like you were telling the truth, kid."

"I didn't kill anybody."

"I know that. A neighborhood pool was hit less than twenty minutes ago. The whole facility, which contained over two hundred people, was brought down. *Systematically* brought down. It was done in such a way its destruction forced people to be inside during the collapse.

Very few escaped and those who did saw Axiom-man on the scene. I was here looking at you when it happened, so unless one of your special tricks is being in two places at once, I have no choice but to believe you've been on the level the whole time. Unless you *can* split yourself in two."

Gabriel wasn't in the mood for this. "What do you think?" *How does he know it's really me? I don't have my costume. Maybe he's thinking of all the gunfire last night. He's probably going off a description of what I was wearing.* He suddenly realized that any number of things could've happened to him while he was under, including the taking of blood, dental casts, fingerprinting, or anything else that could identify him.

"You're lucky you didn't die. Turns out your posterior tibial artery had been knicked. Had you lost any more blood, you would've been a goner."

He didn't say anything, his mind too focused on the possible loss of his secret identity. What would that mean going forward? What about his family? Valerie? His friends?

"How long was I out?" Gabriel asked.

"About a day and a half."

*Did they drug me to keep me under that long?*

"What do you want, Jack? Why are you here?"

Jack stood and put his gun in a holster under his arm, then shoved his hands in his trench coat pockets. "I wanted you to know you're off the hook and that you'll have our co-operation to take down whoever is out there masquerading as you."

"Why the change in heart? Don't you want to hold me on other charges?"

"As much as I'd love to, there are bigger things at stake right now, like that super-powered maniac terrorizing my city. He needs to be stopped."

"I need to get out of here if we're going to do that."

"Doctor says walking might be difficult never mind fighting."

"I'll make do. I need to know not just the Special Force Unit but all of the police will lay off me once I'm out. Whoever is doing this is powerful and any interference from them could jeopardize bringing this person to justice."

"Look, kid, this isn't the time to try and always be the hero."

"I'm not saying you can't help. I'm saying I need to know that your men won't open fire on me."

"You have my word."

He wanted to say Jack would have to do better than that, but it seemed the Special Force Leader was coming around and starting to understand that to keep the city safe, Axiom-man *and* the SFU would have to truly be on the same side.

Or Jack was putting on an incredible show.

Gabriel remembered Katie's caution that Jack wasn't one hundred percent on the level. Perhaps a more cautious alliance would best be in order instead.

He wanted to ask about any possible identifying information having been taken from him, but if nothing had been done, he didn't want to give Jack any ideas either.

A nurse entered the room. She wore scrubs, her black hair done up in a bun, and she wore thick-framed glasses. She was tall, but carried herself with a hunch. Despite the scrubs, Gabriel couldn't help but notice her shapely figure. She told Jack, "Excuse me, sir, but you're going to have to leave."

"I have orders to stay," Jack said.

*Orders?*

"Now that this man is conscious, we'll need to run a few tests," she said. Her voice was timid. She'd have to do better if she was going to stand up to Jack. "Please, the hospital needs your co-operation in this matter."

"Whatever you do to him you can do in front of me," Jack said.

"I'm sorry, sir, but that's not possible. Some matters are . . . more private than others."

"Private, huh?"

"Yes."

Jack showed her his badge. "Very well, but do not let him out of your sight. I'll be outside the door, but he does not leave this room, understood?"

The nurse looked confused. "Where can he go, sir, there's only one door?"

Jack grimaced. "Keep me posted." He left in a huff and slammed the door shut behind him.

The nurse shuddered, then came over to Gabriel, straightening up as she walked, adding at least three inches to her height. He placed her at six-two or six-three. Her movement changed and she carried herself with grace and power. When she leaned over him, her vibrant green eyes shone like emeralds behind her glasses.

---

After about forty-five minutes, Jack was starting to lose it. How long did it take to run a few tests on a patient? It wasn't like the nurse had come in with a tray of items to do so, nor was there anything beyond some intravenous and a couple monitors in the room.

He tried turning the door handle, but it was locked. Jack banged on the door and did his best to keep his composure. "Open the door, please," he said firmly.

The officer standing next to him, one of five guarding the room in case Axiom-man tried anything, banged on the door right after. "Hey!"

"Do you mind?" Jack said. "Just watch the hallway like you're supposed to."

"Sorry," the officer said.

Jack rolled his eyes and banged on the door again. "Open the door!"

Nothing.

"Open the door. This is a police investigation. You must comply."

No answer.

In a rage, Jack grabbed a young orderly walking past.

"Hey, take it easy," the orderly said.

"Open this door," Jack said, pointing to it.

"Sorry?"

Jack grabbed him by the arm and threw him into it.

"Hey, watch it!" the orderly said.

"Open it!"

Clearly intimidated, the orderly fumbled for his key ring and opened the door. Jack shoved him out of the way and went in. He spun on his heels and punched the drywall when he saw that the room was empty.

# Chapter Fifteen

THE NEXT DAY, Valerie was buzzing around Owen Tower like a queen bee on a mission and helped oversee the arrival of everyone ranging from the WPD for security to local politicians, to major CEOs both domestic and foreign, to the press.

Taking a quiet moment to herself, she stepped up to the coffee machine set out in the lobby for the snacks and drinks afterward and poured herself a much-needed cup.

She pulled out her cell and auto-dialed Gabriel's number thinking perhaps he was released from hospital. If he was there. She hoped he hadn't been arrested and was sitting in jail for the past few days. There was no answer. *Please be all right.*

Just as she disconnected the call, her phone rang. It was Mr. Owen.

He said, "I'll be down shortly. Meet me by the south elevator. Bring John and Frank with you. We'll meet the press together." John and Frank were working security at the front, but would then pass off the duties to others so they could act as bodyguards.

"Me?"

"I'm not going to field questions by myself. Some items will need to go through you for follow up. This isn't my first rodeo, Valerie."

"It's mine, though."

"I know, but you've dealt with these people already, just not in a public forum like this. Just stick by me and I'll refer folks to you when needed. See you in a few." He disconnected and Valerie marveled at how calm the man was while she was a nervous wreck.

———

Oscar pulled his charcoal-gray Armani jacket over his frame and double-checked himself in the mirror. The suit sat well, hiding what was beneath.

Today would be a day the city would never forget.

———

The moment Valerie exited the front doors with Mr. Owen and walked up to the red-carpeted platform out front of Owen Tower, her butterflies immediately ceased. This wasn't so bad. All she had to do was stand off to the side while he took the podium, made his introduction, then hand him the giant golden scissors he'd give to the mayor, who would in turn cut the ribbon.

"Ladies and gentlemen of the press, MLAs, Mr. Mayor, and my fellow Winnipeggers, thank you for coming today." He glanced over the audience, which Valerie guessed measured around a thousand attendees. Everyone working in Owen Tower had been invited not to mention all the others outside of it. "Today marks a special day not just for the city, but for myself also. Most importantly, it marks a special day for you. Yes, you. Owen Tower was built as a means to provide extremely affordable office space for not just established businesses, but start-ups. I've long advocated that small business is the lifeblood of any community. My own started off as such, then quickly grew. Now I invite the city to grow along with it. After all, we're in this together." He took a sip of water from the glass behind the podium. "Today marks a day of change." He looked around and smiled at a few of the flashing cameras. "It is my hope that the opening of this tower is a step forward into a bright future for local business and, soon, international business. I want to take this opportunity to announce to the world that plans are underway to construct other high-rises with the same goals in other Canadian cities, all under the Owen Enterprises banner, with doors open for future occupancy to businesses nationwide and abroad."

People whistled and clapped.

Valerie smiled. Even the building of this local high-rise helped out the city by creating over two hundred new jobs just to keep the tower running.

"I don't want to bore you with speeches, however," Oscar said, "so without further ado, I invite you, Mr. Mayor, to come up here and help me cut the ribbon on this place."

The mayor, Charles Jones, stood, smiled and waved to the crowd, then joined Oscar on the platform. The two men shook hands, posed a moment for the cameras, then made their way a few feet back to the front doors, where a ribbon was suspended between two posts.

Valerie motioned to a staff member off to the side and the person went and moved the podium out of the way so people could get a clear view of the two men at the doors. Valerie took its place and instructed the press to come closer but give the men some room, then she stepped off to the side.

The media stampeded forward and Frank and John had to step in between Oscar and the mayor and the crowd to prevent them from getting any closer.

Cameras flashed.

After a brief exchange of words, it seemed the mayor wanted the ribbon cutting to be a co-effort, so together Oscar and Mayor Jones took the scissor handles and brought the blade to the ribbon. With a final glance back over their shoulders the two men smiled at the press, then cut the ribbon together. All looking on erupted in a big cheer and the grinning mayor raised Oscar's hand as if Oscar had just been crowned champion of the city.

Valerie took her spot center stage again and said, "You are all more than welcome to come inside and celebrate. You'll be instructed further as to how to proceed as you enter. Mr. Owen will be off to the side here to answer any questions."

Oscar came up to her.

"Congratulations, sir," she said.

"See, it wasn't so bad," he replied.

She smiled. "No."

They went off to the side. Some of the press followed them while the politicians and other higher-up business types went in.

As Valerie and Oscar waited for the press to gather around, a huge explosion rocked the ground and sent a fireball out the foyer doors. Bodies and debris went flying back, smoke and dust filling the air. With a yelp, Valerie ducked and put her palms over her head to protect herself. People shouted and screamed.

Coughing, Valerie got to her feet and looked for her boss.

He was gone.

She stood on her tiptoes, trying to get a look over the crowd. John and Frank had already joined other members of the security team to help with crowd control, same with the WPD.

What just happened?

Valerie rounded to the front of the building, stepping over chunks of concrete, metal and glass. She gasped when she saw the first body—Jill, someone who worked in her office—face bloodied, with sharp shards of cement and a deformed piece of rebar sticking out of her chest.

Tears welling up from the sight, Valerie guarded herself against all those shoving past her, trying to get some distance from the building.

To her left, a familiar figure emerged from the blown-out doors and a jolt shot through her.

"Axiom-man," she said. *How'd he get inside?*

The man in blue stepped forward through the wreckage. Some members of the media clicked their cameras. A flush of relief came over the faces of some, while sheer terror rocked the faces of others.

Valerie was about to give him a wave when a young girl came up to him. She looked no more than twelve.

"Help me! I can't find my mom," the girl said.

Axiom-man looked at her then picked her up under her armpits. The girl's body started to shake and smoke started to rise beneath her arms. Soon, the convulsions increased and she began to squeal.

In the distance, a loud rush of wind rose on the air, getting louder and louder. From the side, a streak of blue rushed in and the girl was yanked from Axiom-man's arms, the gust of wind from whatever it was carrying a trail of dust and smoke with it.

A moment later, Valerie heard a familiar voice behind her. "You need to get somewhere safe."

She spun around and set her eyes on glowing blue ones. His costume was fresh, clean, his light blue cape hanging over his shoulders like a king's robe. "Axiom-man?"

"It's me, Valerie. Now get out of here. We'll catch up later."

Trembling, then glancing back at the other Axiom-man, she started away, careful not to lose her footing on the chunks of concrete on the ground.

Axiom-man—*her* Axiom-man—gave her a nod as she walked off then reaffixed his gaze on the menace before him.

———

It felt so good to be back in his old costume, like coming home and discovering who he really was and what he was meant to do for the first time all over again.

Axiom-man eyed the imposter in front of him, letting blue energy fill his eyes. Fists clenched, he started walking toward him. "You have killed innocent people. You have destroyed public and private property. You have ruined my name. I'm bringing you down."

"Really?" the man in blue said. "You're welcome to try."

*You're welcome to try?* Axiom-man thought.

The man in blue stepped a few paces over to the side next to a large chunk of concrete debris. He quickly bent down, picked it up, and hurled it at Axiom-man. Axiom-man dove out of the way as the giant chunk of concrete sped past and crashed into a news van behind him.

Axiom-man rushed him. This wasn't a time for mercy.

The man in blue grabbed hold of him with a vice-like grip, then threw him over his hips to the ground. The man jumped on him and brought a fist into Axiom-man's face. The blow irritated his already-injured eyes, but the aura seemed to have absorbed some of the impact. Jerking his hips, Axiom-man bucked under him and shot the man onto his chest so he could then bend and get his legs up and around the man from behind and throw him downward. His legs locked on under the man's arms and he gave it everything he had, slamming the guy down against the concrete. Axiom-man rolled off him and got to his feet, and before the other guy could get to his own, Axiom-man brought his foot down on the man's stomach. The man let out a gasp, jerked his body and punched Axiom-man square in the knee. Axiom-man's leg buckled; it was the same leg recovering from the bullet wound. He used his other leg to maintain his balance and hovered slightly off the ground, reminding himself that he'd have to stay airborne from now on unless he wanted to find himself on his back again.

The man in blue tried to grab him but Axiom-man floated high enough to avoid the man's hands. Below, the other guy got to his feet and flew up after him.

*He can fly?* Axiom-man thought. What was he dealing with here? A by-product of the black clouds again? Something else?

They ascended higher into the sky. The man in blue came up beside him and took a swing. Axiom-man avoided the blow and delivered one of his own, his fist meaning to connect with the man's head but the guy suddenly changed levels and it connected with his shoulder instead. The force of the blow was enough to send the guy turning, but then he doubled back around and clocked Axiom-man square in the cheekbone. Pain lit up his face and he yelled from the strike.

Diving into him, Axiom-man got his hands around the man's waist and started to push against him, scanning the streets below for a place to take him down and, hopefully, take him out. He had to do it quickly as his injured hand was only operating at half-strength. The man brought his fists down on Axiom-man's back, forcing him to lose his grip and fall several inches before grabbing onto the man's thighs. In a quick aerial move, the man arced back upside down, flipping Axiom-man off his legs like a boulder from a catapult. Axiom-man tumbled through the air, slowed himself, then turned mid-air to face his target.

He wasn't behind him anymore.

*He's really adept at flying,* Axiom-man thought, thinking back to when he first learned to fly it took a little while to get the hang of it, then, after that, even more time to do it fluidly, mastering aerial maneuvers and steering until it became second nature. Even after this recent surge, he had to teach himself how to operate efficiently at a higher speed.

What felt like a battering ram hit him from behind, square in the shoulder blades. Axiom-man's back locked and his arms went snapping out to the side from the impact, his head going back. Whiplash.

Body locking from the shock, he turned and saw the heel of a dark blue boot coming for his face. He killed his flight and dropped from the air, the boot missing him. Once out of harm's way, he activated his flight again, flew a safe distance and turned around to face his quarry and reassess. The man in blue was already flying after him, fists punched out before him.

Axiom-man's breath caught in his throat when he noticed the man's fists glow red.

# Chapter Sixteen

THE MAN IN blue's fists pulsed with red energy, the crimson glow growing bigger and brighter the closer he flew toward Axiom-man.

"Redsaw," Axiom-man said. He'd had his suspicions, but there had been no way to prove it until now. Axiom-man let his eyes fill with blue energy and kept close watch on the man's fists. He'd felt those blasts before and it was painful every time.

The man flew closer and let the red energy shoot from his hands. Axiom-man met it head-on with a blast from his eye beams. The two power beams collided mid-air in a brilliant blast of crackling, electric purple. Gritting his teeth, Axiom-man kept pumping the energy out, sensing the red beams resisting it on the other end. He'd forgotten how strong Redsaw was and how even his eye beams had to struggle to make a dent.

*Why didn't I sense him this time?* he wondered. He considered the blue aura on his skin. Perhaps it shielded him from Redsaw's presence. Maybe those days of feeling like his power was draining around his old enemy were a thing of the past. It was a good thing . . . but it also made Redsaw invisible to him if he wasn't looking right at him. No more warning or chance for a pre-emptive attack.

The two men flew at each other, the energy beams between them growing more intense. When they almost collided, they veered off, arced around, then came out, energy firing again. Blue and red power smashed into each other in the sky and Axiom-man could only imagine what it looked like to those watching below.

———

Valerie stood on the street corner, looking up, hand above her eyes to shield them from the sun's glare as she saw the blue, red and purple fireworks in the sky.

"Redsaw's back," she said. *Come on, Gabriel, you can take him. You have to.* Redsaw was a menace worse than any petty criminal, worse than even Bleaken. She remembered the chaos he caused that night in the MTS Centre and all the suffering. She remembered the killing streak that led up to it. Was that evil man doing the same thing now albeit under the guise of Axiom-man? Or was it simply his aim to tarnish Axiom-man's name and drive him underground? If so, he should've known it would take a lot more than that to stop Gabriel.

Gabriel—Axiom-man—wouldn't give up.

Not without a fight.

———

Axiom-man'd had a lot of practice since last encountering Redsaw, not just in the flight department, but also in using his energy beams as an extension of himself, like an extra set of limbs. Plus he'd also recently had a surge, which gave him an advantage as Redsaw had always been the stronger of the two. Yet he noticed Redsaw seemed fresh and more powerful than he remembered, so either his memory was fuzzy or the time away actually did Redsaw some good in the power department. Regardless, he couldn't let the man go, and with Jack Gunn and the SFU claiming to have facilities to hold those with special abilities, there would be a place to lock up Redsaw once this was over and keep him there for good.

He had to answer for all the lives he had stolen.

The man in the blue suit came in hard and fast and Axiom-man couldn't stand looking at a mirror image of himself charging toward him any longer. He flew at him just as hard, eyes lit up, and as he flew past, he fired off a series of energy beams that caught the man in the chest and face. The man slowed his flight and Axiom-man glanced back over his shoulder. The man reached down and tore the blue fabric off his chest and face, then ripped at the entire outfit until it hung off him like rags, revealing the sleek, red and black Redsaw costume underneath. A long black cape hung over his shoulders, and when he turned around, Axiom-man saw the familiar half mask and the adjoining jagged black band that ran down red-clad legs all the way to his feet.

The two men floated in the air, staring at each other.

"You will pay for what you did, Redsaw," Axiom-man said.

"Good to see you, too, Axiom-man. It's been a long time."

"You should have stayed away."

"I was never away."

"Yes, you—" He caught himself and realized Redsaw meant that though the menace might not've been out in costume, he'd been working on something away from the public eye. "Come with me."

"Oh really? Where? To Jack Gunn and the 'Special' Force headquarters? The WPD? Do you really think that could hold me?"

"We're about to find out." Axiom-man flew at him, eyes blazing, and let off repeated pulses of energy.

Redsaw immediately went into action and dodged around the blasts before swooping straight down then coming back up and plowing his fists into Axiom-man's stomach. Axiom-man's insides lurched and he thought he was about to lose his lunch. His face hurt like crazy and his eyes were beginning to swell shut. He'd be taking a long bath in a tub full of ice once this was over.

Axiom-man went to fire with his eyes, but Redsaw came in with a left hook then a right one, sending his head snapping one way then the next, dazing him. The blue aura seemed to be absorbing some of the shock of the blows, but not nearly enough to make him brush them off. Dizzy, Axiom-man came back with a haymaker that connected with Redsaw's mouth, drawing blood.

Redsaw turned tail and flew toward the city below.

*No, got to keep him away.* He remembered the last time the two tangled on the city streets and the destruction it wrought. He couldn't let it happen again. Axiom-man followed suit, kicking on the speed and reveling in how much faster he was and how quickly he was gaining air on his enemy.

Redsaw landed at a construction site, slamming down onto a pile of plywood, sending the boards up in a rain of splinters. Axiom-man brought up his guard to shield himself from taking any shards in the eyes as he sped through the falling debris and crashed into Redsaw, sending them both tumbling across the ground. They came to a stop mid-site. Redsaw was on top of him and punched down. Axiom-man moved, Redsaw's fist catching the side of his neck. It made him gasp. Had he been slugged dead-on, the blow would've no doubt crushed his windpipe. Axiom-man pulled his legs in quick and tight, driving his knees into Redsaw's back, and sent the man sprawling forward on top of him. Redsaw scrambled off, bent down, and grabbed Axiom-man by the shoulders, picking him up and throwing him head over heels into a cement foundation some thirty feet deep. Axiom-man kicked on his flight before hitting the ground, stopped himself, turned over and made to fly out and into Redsaw, but was met with a powerful blast of red energy to his chest that took the air from his lungs and sent him falling back to his knees. Legs screaming, he thought the impact had broken his kneecaps. He managed to float off the ground and slowly lower his legs under himself. Each move of the joints made his muscles ache, especially those of his damaged leg.

He couldn't see Redsaw over the horizon of the foundation hole. He brought up his guard, ready for anything—

—except the cement truck that came flying over the edge.

The last image he saw was its grime-covered barrel heading right at him. He fired off a blast of energy from his eyes. The barrel split in two, one half crashing into him. He passed through the thick liquid cement within before slamming up against the barrel's interior. He bounced off, flipped over, and hit the ground. Now on his stomach, the last thing he saw as he lost consciousness was a river of liquid cement coming toward him.

———

The two titans disappeared over the top of the buildings a few minutes back and Valerie didn't know where they went. She hoped Axiom-man had managed to take the battle away from the city, but at the rate Redsaw was coming at him, she didn't know how well he'd be able to pull it off. Axiom-man seemed to have a pretty good handle on combat and certainly had the advantage when going up against anyone weaker than him, but when it came going toe-to-toe with someone just as powerful or even more so, she wasn't sure how he'd hold up or what leg up he might have. Never mind the injuries he'd endured from the SFU. She wasn't an aggressive person herself and with the more trials and dangers she'd undergone, the more she hated violence and the destruction it brought.

She wandered back to the Owen Tower site and stood there staring at the front of the newly-constructed building. The whole lower section had been blown out, taking the walls and glass with it. Support beams remained, keeping the structure up. Rubble was everywhere. Police questioned witnesses and firemen put out fires. The paramedics were still rounding up the bodies, some being loaded onto ambulances, others joining a lengthy row of them while they waited their turn for transport.

Reporters and news crews surrounded the perimeter of the building. The police had managed to tape off all the danger spots with only emergency crews allowed to enter. Valerie recognized some familiar faces in the surrounding crowd as people who worked elsewhere in the building.

Where was Mr. Owen?

*Probably locked up in a panic room somewhere,* she thought. *Was Redsaw's attack personal or just random?*

The very thought of Redsaw being back made Valerie's skin crawl, and she knew once the rest of the populace caught wind of it, the whole city would be in a state of unrest. She hoped that Axiom-man would be more equipped to deal with Redsaw this time around, same with the City. Before, both Axiom-man and Redsaw were new on the scene and the world wasn't ready for super-powered people to exist. As commendable as their response was, the police were easily outmatched and outgunned against those with special abilities.

She pulled out her cellphone and dialed Gabriel's number. She knew he wasn't home but wanted to leave him a message. After the beep, she said, "Hi, it's me. Call me as soon as you get this as I want to make sure you're okay. I'm worried about you. I don't want to say too much on the phone, but you know what I'm talking about. Please, please call me when you get a chance." She paused a moment, thinking maybe she should say more, but instead ended the call. She didn't know if he wanted to hear the mushy stuff just now with all that was happening.

Valerie did her best to push her worry for him out of her mind and scrolled through her address book to find Mr. Owen's cell number. She didn't know what the protocol was on something like this.

---

Axiom-man was curled up when he awoke, his arm stuck in heavy sludge, his cape drawn over him. He must've pulled the material over top of him to shield himself from the liquid cement before blacking out. It hadn't dried, but was well on its way to doing so, which indicated a decent amount of time had passed since he lost consciousness. The way his cape was situated with his arm outstretched created a makeshift canopy thus a pocket of air. How much was left for him to use, he wasn't sure, but it was as hot as the dickens in here and he noticed his breathing was already forcibly shallow from the $CO_2$ build-up.

The heavy cement on him was crushing, putting pressure on his legs, ribs and back. The back of his head felt like it was in a vice whereas the pressure got lighter closer toward the front of his skull. He wanted to take a deep breath, but forced himself to conserve whatever air he had remaining and formulate a plan.

He *shifted* and activated his powers. The pressure against his head and body lessened and it became clear what the strange light blue aura on his skin was: a force field. It wasn't an impenetrable one, but it was quickly becoming a big help. He recalled the messenger's words to him about his powers, how the surges worked and why. It seemed the more responsible he was with his abilities and the more he applied them, the more was given unto him. Getting a force field aura was never anything he expected, but he was thankful it was helping him now, even just a little. He could only imagine what it might become if he continued down the right path with his abilities, but he couldn't dwell on that now.

Axiom-man wiggled beneath the heavy cement and could only guess the combined weight spread over his body was a couple thousand pounds or more. This meant that either the aura was so strong it was able to support that weight or that piece of the cement barrel was still above him in such a way that the liquid cement covered him and encased him in a Twinkie-like fashion, him inside a partial metal barrel with concrete filling. It was the latter, now that he thought about it. Had it not been, he would've been crushed before regaining consciousness.

He lit up his eyes to a faint glow so he could see in the dark. All he saw was wet cement in his immediate line of sight, his arm stretched out by his head only visible to halfway down his bicep before disappearing beneath dark gray cement. His other arm was stretched out along with this cape, which was sunken in places, only partly visible as well. His legs were drawn up and it was difficult to move.

Summoning all this strength, he tried to push himself away from the ground but was unable to budge the weight above him. Growling, he tried again to the same result. Whatever was bearing down on him passed even his own lifting threshold.

"Okay, think," he whispered. *Not strong enough to budge this thing.* There was only one option and that was to cut his way out with his eye beams, but where to start? He glanced around and since his head was locked in place thanks to the cement pressing on it, his line of sight was directly at his arms. He could try to cut away the cement around them, but the cement was also still spongy so it'd be like cutting through Jell-O: nothing would really break away. Perhaps his eye beams could dry the cement, but if so, the temperature it would create would burn his arms encased within and he didn't know if the aura would protect against that.

"I'm trapped," he said. Just then his heart started racing and he wished he had his cellphone and some sort of auto-dialer built into his mask. He could then call for outside help, be dug up and get on with stopping Redsaw.

Furious, Axiom-man struggled against his cement tomb, holding his breath for the longest intervals he could manage, trying not to use up whatever little air he had left.

# Chapter Seventeen

Late that night, Redsaw soared through the air, reveling in his victory. His triumphant return hadn't panned out exactly the way he wanted—he had hoped for a more dramatic entrance after tarnishing Axiom-man's reputation even more—but he decided to make do with what he had.

Thanks to a well-placed and well-hidden pack of explosives, he had been able to trigger the explosion at the base of Owen Tower from a controller in his pocket, making it look like Axiom-man did it. And by having Oscar Owen in plain view when it happened, it further ensured that Oscar was in no way related to these powerful men terrorizing the city. Besides, the insurance money gained from the explosion was more than the damage actually caused and would only line his pockets further to help fund the additional towers currently planned.

And they were needed.

Each tower would serve as a series of fresh access points to new Doorw—

Gunshots sounded, bullets ripping past him. He scanned the rooftops below and saw at least two laser sights coming from every other rooftop all over downtown.

*Smart,* he thought. *Got to give the Special Force Unit more credit.* Perhaps they *were* learning and were willing to meet those like him with deadly force.

Redsaw immediately unleashed a fireball of red energy at the first of the snipers, the beam striking the man in the face and sending him to the ground. The second gunman on the roof opened fire and Redsaw flew in a spiraling arc to confuse the shot before sending down a zap of red power into the man's neck, severing his head from his body. Redsaw landed on the roof and got behind a ventilation bulkhead. On the rooftop across the way were two others, and if he remembered their positioning correctly, they were very close together. He jumped out from behind the bulkhead and fired off a stream of red energy from his hands to the rooftop across from him. He crisscrossed his hands then parted them a few times, the red beam slicing through the air and anything in its path like a death ray. Once done, he jumped into the air and got to the rooftop with the men in one leap and verified the kills.

The sound of an approaching chopper—no, *two* choppers—rose on the air and soon a set of spotlights were upon him. Bullets rained down. To protect himself, Redsaw radiated red energy from his raised hands, letting it build and build until its ambient power stood over him like a crimson umbrella. The bullets hitting it burst as they passed through and were rendered harmless. He kept moving, avoiding any micro shrapnel from the bullets before launching into the air and landing on the skid of one of the helicopters. With a powerful blast of his fist, he cut through the chopper's flooring, slaughtering all who were inside. He released himself from the chopper as it started to go down and quickly flew to the next, this time letting himself plow straight through the glass and into the cockpit, his fists driving into the pilot's chest with such force he penetrated the ribcage. Blood gushed everywhere when he tore his hands out and sent a blast of fiery red power into the face of the co-pilot. Two gunmen were at the back of the chopper, adjusting their stances to face the front and aim their weapons. Before they could fire, Redsaw back flipped out of the cockpit window as the chopper began to fall from the sky. A loud crash sounded as the first chopper slammed into a rooftop. Not content with letting the SFU agents in the second chopper simply fall to their deaths, he flew in from the side, the cabin door already open, gunmen shooting. Once again, he used the red energy as a shield and sent a pulse of it outward, obliterating the men within. The chopper spun out of control and struck the side of a building before tumbling off and smashing into the street in a fireball.

More gunshots came from the surrounding rooftops. Redsaw kept an erratic flight pattern to avoid getting hit. He would show this city, the WPD, the SFU, even the military should they try and intervene, that he was a force to be reckoned with and even their best tricks wouldn't stop him. They would learn the difference between him and Axiom-man, and he was all too willing to teach them.

He flew over one rooftop and zapped the gunmen on top then came streaking to another, grabbed one gunman by the neck, dragged him off the rooftop, let go and made the man fall to his doom. He zapped the other stunned sniper looking on, ending him.

It was going to be a wild night.

———

The cement was drying quickly and Axiom-man couldn't move. Sweating and in the dark, he pushed and pressed against the concrete cocoon.

He'd stop shouting for assistance half an hour ago. The air was almost gone and the little he did get into his lungs wasn't enough to ward off the ringing in his ears and the green fuzziness rimming his vision.

This was it.

He was going to die.

"Messenger, help me . . ." He could barely form the words.

The minutes passed and he began to lose heart with each helpless second.

He wondered what it'd be like for the person who found him come morning. Odds were the construction workers building the site would see the mess and start cleaning things up. Eventually they'd have to break apart the pile of concrete and the embedded cement truck barrel so they could haul it away. Would they find him by seeing his appendages sticking out from between the chunks of cement, or would he be part of a concrete block of its own that got hauled away and they would be none the wiser?

Redsaw would overtake the city and the world would no doubt fall under his shadow soon after.

He started to tremble, a combination of nerves and anger. He was about to face death, and though he'd played the scenario over in his mind now and then, it was the moment of death he wondered about most. Did things go dark and then . . . a bright light? What if he went to the other place? Would fire burst up around him and cover him in flames? Would he see the messenger? An angel? God?

How much would he be remembered?

The vibrations of his quaking traveled right to his core and when he went to breathe again, there wasn't any more air left.

His eyes went wide at the realization, but the swelling muted the reaction. Desperate, he lashed out with a blast of energy from his eyes and the power of the beam shot through the cement, sending shards of it backward at his face. The beam struck his hand and though he felt its sting, the aura seemed to have absorbed most of it. Now he had chunks of concrete pressed up against his face, its dust coating his tongue in a muddy sludge.

Shaking, he pressed his arms against the cement, not caring if he brought the whole thing down on himself. *If* it even moved, that was. He was as good as dead anyway.

Axiom-man pressed outward with his arms, then pushed inward with his palms, shifting the force back and forth, back and forth, giving it all he had, lungs screaming for air, panic raging through him, heart pounding, hope fading until . . .

. . . a blast of vigor and enthusiasm spiked through him, a dump of endless energy filling him, working from his core outward. The concrete began to crack and give way around him, his arms moving through the near-dry cement, at first slowly then picking up pace. It grew lighter and lighter, and when he went to push his palms against the ground, they actually dug into the concrete beneath him as he gave it all he had.

At first he thought he hadn't really tapped his true potential when he first tried to escape, but this feeling of losing influence over his abilities, of the strength taking over, was akin to the same one he felt when he lost control as he soared higher and faster into the sky the other night.

This was another surge . . . and it was enhancing his strength.

Axiom-man exerted himself, pushing his body against what had to be a ton and a half of weight against him, the chunk of metal barrel from the cement truck included. He slowly managed to get his legs under him and gave it all he had, pressing his heels into the ground and expelling every last ounce of air he'd held in his lungs. He bore the cement slab's weight on his shoulders and finally stood. Once standing, his arms now free, chunks of cement clinging to him, he bent his arms at the elbows and got his palms beneath the slab. With a giant push, he threw it off him. The thing flew into the air at least a hundred feet before crashing down thirty or forty feet away somewhere outside of the foundation hole.

He stood there shaking before rising out of the hole and getting a good look at the weight that was on him. It *was* half the barrel from the truck, bigger than he recalled. Most of the cement that had encased him was still attached to it and ran at least four feet thick.

Shaking from the surge of power and natural adrenaline, he started to cough and hack, getting the cement dust out of his mouth and lungs and finally, oh finally, getting a lungful of air. He stood there just gasping and choking and . . . breathing. Finally. Breathing.

He grabbed at the chunks of cement still clinging to him and crushed them with his fingers, getting them off. They burst between his fingertips like damp sand.

The surge wouldn't last much longer, which was too bad because to unleash it on Redsaw would make stopping the maniac so much easier.

One thing was for certain, however: he had to find him.

Valerie had kept her eyes glued to the television screen late into the night. All the major networks were covering the aftermath of the two Axiom-mans fighting, many of the stations from around the globe sending in news crews by the hour.

Rumors of Redsaw's return had quickly spread and fearful headlines were popping up all over the Internet. The big question on everyone's mind was: where was Axiom-man? He had gone missing hours ago and hadn't surfaced since. Some had feared the worst, others thought the Cobalt Crusader had gone off somewhere to regroup and formulate a plan. Others thought the two super-powered beings were duking it out in an unknown location.

Valerie had left a second message for Gabriel about an hour ago, begging him to call her. Her stomach was in knots and she even thought about going to his place and checking up on him in case he had gotten hurt and was there recovering. But to make it there . . . . Riots had started up and random acts of arson despite the curfew. Having seen—and experienced—the animals that come out during a time of crisis before, she had no choice but to stay indoors.

The latest story was a massacre downtown. Local police and the SFU were at a loss. Redsaw had slaughtered every man on the rooftops whose job it was to shoot the flying villain down. That evil man was making a statement, that much was certain. The whole city was on lockdown with the TV, Internet and radio all demanding citizens remain indoors until further notice. Even the phone companies sent out a mass text to all their users, advising them of the same. Valerie didn't know these companies could do that.

She had checked her work email from home since she couldn't go back to the office after what happened. Her inbox was flooded with inquiries from the news networks, city workers, tenants, laymen and others, all asking pretty much the same question: was the tower done for and was everyone okay? She hadn't heard from

Mr. Owen so she didn't have an answer. She just hoped her boss was all right.

———

Redsaw flew to the roof of Owen Tower and looked out across the city. Fires burned, sirens wailed, and those foolish enough to be on the streets were actually rioting and looting from the chaos, keeping the cops plenty busy.

"Welcome home," he said to himself. Ever since his killing spree started, he felt himself growing more and more powerful, the red energy within growing and bubbling beneath the surface. After destroying all those who had tried to shoot him down, he felt like the power within was bursting at the seams and begging to be let loose. He briefly considered right here, right now, opening a new Doorway, but what for? There was no need to connect with his master at the moment. Not while he was having so much fun and not before the other towers were set up. Besides, if he could learn to keep the energy within at bay and use it and control it—he would be invincible.

Fighting Axiom-man—something was different about him. Axiom-man seemed stronger than the last time they tangled. When they had fought before, the difference in strength had been noticeable, but now . . . it was close. Very close, and, at times during the encounter, it seemed Axiom-man was holding back and could really let him have it if he wanted to.

"It can't be," Redsaw said. "Need to make sure he's no longer a threat." He remembered why he hadn't killed Axiom-man the night the Doorway of Darkness opened and the fear of facing whoever gave Axiom-man his power. But now, after all these deaths and the incredible strength they birthed within him, Redsaw felt like he could take on anyone or anything, including this strange otherworldly force, if it came to it.

He flew off in the direction of the construction site. When he arrived, he was dismayed to see the foundation hole not as he left it. A broken cement truck barrel sat caked in concrete outside the hole. Axiom-man had clearly escaped. He had thought the sheer weight of it all would've crushed him. He wasn't invincible, was he? That wasn't the case last time unless his nemesis somehow developed that as a new ability.

"No!" Redsaw shouted.

Now that he was back, he couldn't have Axiom-man interfere with his plans. There was only one way to ensure that.

# CHAPTER EIGHTEEN

Valerie finally turned the TV off around 2:30 and made her way to the bathroom to get ready for bed. As she brushed her teeth, she heard a tap on the glass of her balcony window.

*Gabriel!* "Thank goodness," she said, then spat in the sink, quickly wiped her mouth and ran for the window. She yelped when she pulled back the curtain. A black-gloved fist burst through the glass and grabbed her by the throat.

———

Axiom-man spent the last couple of hours looking for Redsaw, but to no avail. He had stepped in on a few escalating riots on the streets, assisting the tired cops. He did overhear an officer say anyone caught out of their homes were to be immediately detained regardless of what they were doing. How they actually hoped to stay on top of all their arrests despite being vastly outnumbered was another issue.

"How am I supposed to find him?" Axiom-man asked himself. *It's the same as before: just aimless flying around. I don't have some magnifying vision that lets me see every detail and every person on every street.* He wondered if that was an ability he would develop in the future, maybe at the next surge. *No, the surges seem to be an enhancement of what you already have.* Even the aura was an extension of his eyes beams and emanated from there.

"Maybe I should just check in with Jack," he said, then remembered how mad Jack probably was thanks to his disappearing act at the hospital. *That nurse* . . . "I don't think Jack'd try and detain me, though. Not after today. Not after fighting Redsaw." *Jack knew I was innocent before that, but today would've really proven it.*

He flew off in the direction of the police station and hoped Jack was in.

----

Jack Gunn sat at his desk, staring at the stack of reports that came in over the past half hour. He looked up when a young female officer dropped another handful on his desk. They were casualty reports, all men killed in the line of duty, many from his department. On the surface, planting snipers across the city's rooftops seemed like a good way to lockdown the skies under Operation Rogue. Even the military had been behind it and flew in their top men from Canadian Forces Bases all over the country. Who could outrun—out*fly*—a bullet? Axiom-man and Redsaw, apparently. As good of a shot these men were, and while they certainly could hit a moving target, they weren't trained to hit moving targets that had unlimited range and traversed quicker than cars on a highway.

Now dozens of them were dead.

There was a tap on the window behind him. Jack pulled his gun, spun in his chair, and pointed it at the window. When he saw Axiom-man floating behind the glass with his arms crossed, he approached with caution. This could be Redsaw in disguise.

Jack opened the window but kept the gun trained on him. "Don't mind my paranoia."

"So you won't mind if I don't come in."

"What do you want?"

"Jack, it's me."

"Prove it."

"You were in my hospital room when I came to."

No way Redsaw knew that. "You pulled a Houdini on me and I was none too happy about it. Am still not."

"Had to be done. Listen, you and I need to come to an agreement. I'm on your side, Jack."

"How'd you get out of the hospital?"

"That's a story for another time."

"Tell me now."

"You don't want to hear it."

"That nurse . . ."

"Jack, I need your help. Like I said, I'm on your side."

Jack wanted to believe him, but how could anyone trust someone so powerful? Axiom-man seemed as human as the next guy aside from the special abilities. If that was indeed the case, then he was just as susceptible to the negative sides of human behavior, same as anyone else. Jack knew his own dark side and could only imagine what would happen if special powers ever mingled with it. If Axiom-man had the same inclinations or even similar—even buried deep down—then he could one day be an extremely dangerous person. However, he had thought that day came just recently, but had been proven wrong. "Where is Redsaw?" he asked instead.

"That's why I'm here. I've been looking for him and can't find him anywhere. I was hoping you would know something."

Jack still held the gun high. Axiom-man seemed remarkably calm considering he had the barrel pointed straight at his face. "All I know is that maniac just wiped out an entire squad of men on the city's rooftops."

"I'm acquainted with them."

Jack could detect a bit of anger in Axiom-man's voice when he mentioned the snipers. "I was just doing my job."

"I'm aware."

"Well, you don't need to fear anymore. Redsaw's taken them out and now I have a stack of reports on my desk four inches high and growing, never mind a long list of families to notify."

Axiom-man was silent before saying, "I'm sorry for the loss of your men."

Jack lowered the barrel. "You need to find him. We can hold him here."

"You never did show me what you have on hand."

*Wouldn't you like to know.* "There was never occasion. You bring him in, we can contain him. We've tested our holding cell and unless Redsaw's plenty powerful beyond even our wildest ideas, he's not breaking out. We've had that Bleaken character detained ever since he covered the city in that black cloud. If we can hold him, we can hold Redsaw."

"Redsaw's a different breed of villain altogether. Bleaken was a broken man and quite possibly is simply allowing you to contain him because he's given up. Be on your toes, Jack. There are forces at play that are unlike anything this world is equipped to deal with."

"Enlighten me."

"Perhaps one day if our level of communication improves."

"You want to build trust yet aren't willing to talk."

"Trust is earned, Jack, and I'd hoped I'd earned yours by everything I've done . . . yet you still thought I had turned on everyone."

"It was a mistake."

"I'll extend this olive branch to you: I need an ally, a *real* ally, and I'd like it to be you, but there are many things that need ironing out before that can happen. Perhaps in time."

The comment hit Jack hard. Axiom-man genuinely seemed a good guy beneath that mask, but this was the real world and not the comic books. People weren't mapped out from start to finish with rules about how they could or could not behave. Things turned on a dime in the real world, the same world that was not the same place it used to be thanks to the arrival of these super-powered people. Skepticism and caution were the order of the day. Couple that with those higher in authority breathing down his neck to do things a certain way and it made his job even more complicated.

"Perhaps," Jack said. He sighed and holstered his weapon. "Here." He went to his desk and pulled a small radio unit out of his drawer. He gave it to Axiom-man. "When you find him, radio me and I'll show up ready to detain him. If I find him first, I'll notify you."

Axiom-man took the radio, flipped it around in his fingers and affixed the clip on its back to his belt. "Thanks."

"Now get out of here. Don't want to enjoy each other too much now."

Axiom-man gave a slight nod then reached up and flew into the sky.

"Freak," Jack said as he closed the window. "Just glad he's on our side."

———

*That was completely unfruitful,* Axiom-man thought. Well, that wasn't entirely true. He did get that radio so there was comfort in knowing he'd have backup if needed.

He promised himself he wouldn't rest until he found Redsaw, but he was quickly growing weary of flying around and not making any headway in that regard.

He decided to fly home and scan the headlines. Perhaps something happened that Jack hadn't caught wind of yet but the press had? It was a long shot but anything was worth a try right now. When he got in, he hit the computer. He scanned his inbox, but found nothing other than reports on the hit at the Owen Tower opening ceremony.

Valerie.

He needed to call her and had been too busy to check his messages. She was probably sleeping right now, but with all the chaos and danger, he needed to know she was okay.

"This sucks," he said and brought his fists down on the computer desk. He heard the desk crack from the blow; he hadn't meant to strike it so hard. *Great. Can't find Redsaw and now I just broke my desk and I don't even have a job to help me pay for a new one.* Frustrated, he moved to turn the system off when his monitor started to glow.

"The messenger," Axiom-man said.

# CHAPTER NINETEEN

IT WAS HAPPENING again.

Valerie sat tied to a chair, blood dripping off her nose, tears leaking from her eyes. She didn't know where she was other than the room had wooden boards for walls. The strong scent of pine pinched her nose. The only light was the moonlight coming in through the cracks in the boards.

She sat there, sweat-soaked skin shivering.

And there was no way to contact Gabriel.

Redsaw had grabbed her from her apartment and brought her here, knocked her around then left her tied up. She heard screams, the cries of men, women and children. Maybe they were on someone's property away from the city? That would explain the crickets and lack of city sounds, but with the curfew in effect, city sounds would be near non existent anyway save those rioters and looters who panicked because of the lockdown.

Why did Redsaw kidnap her? Did Mr. Owen somehow cross him and the easiest way to get to him was to kidnap her? Otherwise, the only other thing she could think of aside from plain rotten luck was that he knew she was friends with Axiom-man. How he knew or to what extent, she didn't know. Somehow, he figured it out, tracked her down and . . .

*He's going to use me to lure Axiom-man here. Oh, Gabriel, I'm so sorry.* "I'm so sorry."

After what happened to her when those men kidnapped her and she was locked in that basement, she couldn't bear to go through it again. All those terrible things those men did was nothing compared to what Redsaw was capable of.

———————

Every time the messenger materialized he took Axiom-man's breath away. He was a being of pure, bright blue energy, featureless yet perfectly proportioned and a powerful presence emanated from him at all times.

He stood before Axiom-man, the light radiating off his body illuminating the apartment's front room.

"I've been trying to reach you," Axiom-man said.

"I know. It has been a long time, and I am pleased to see how you are developing."

"Another surge happened."

"I know. You always forget, but we are connected."

*Right.* "Will there be another?"

"That depends on you."

Talking to the messenger this time around wasn't as intimidating. Maybe he was getting used to him? Or maybe this new increase in power gave him more confidence. Either way, it was good to see his old . . . he wouldn't necessarily call him a friend. A mentor would be more accurate though the messenger did leave him to figure out pretty much everything for himself and served more as a guide than a teacher. He also realized the messenger's involvement seemed to be partly based on stewardship and the more he was responsible, the more was revealed to him.

"Redsaw has returned," Axiom-man said.

"And his power is growing. Unlike before, he hasn't exercised the power he's accumulated and it is being stored up in him."

"Exercised?"

"He had used the power he gained from the deaths of others to open the Doorway of Darkness. By doing so, it expelled that energy and drained him. He wasn't powerless, to be sure, but the enhancements he gained through his previous time killing others was vanquished. Now I sense something else is happening and I've come to warn you."

"Of?"

"Dark days are coming unless Redsaw can be stopped. You already know of your destiny to fight him and with the recent surge you stand a better chance of accomplishing that."

This wasn't what Axiom-man wanted to hear. Though he was well aware of one day there being a final showdown between him and Redsaw, he hadn't expected it to happen so soon. He had hoped Redsaw—if he was to eventually resurface—would stay hidden for much longer than he had.

"Am I strong enough?"

The messenger didn't answer, but instead said, "I have sent you an ally, of whom you have already met."

He didn't know if the image of the nurse from the hospital had been telepathically transmitted or if it was simply her image donning on him, but Axiom-man said, "Where is she now?"

"She is fulfilling her duties to me elsewhere, one of which is ensuring all record of your stay at the hospital is neutralized along with the blood samples and fingerprints they took while you were unconscious."

He had forgotten about his concern about that, but to hear it had been taken care of was a relief. "Thanks. Was it Jack?"

"No."

"Then who?"

"You need to be more careful. Part of your mission is to keep this planet shielded from the powers at play. You have done well to contain them and I commend you for that, but you must learn to recognize them when they surface so as to neutralize them before they come to fruition."

"I don't understand."

"As your abilities develop, so will your capability in discerning what is and what is not of this world."

*Now I'm confused.* "Are you saying—"

"Your friend is in danger, the one whom knows your secret."

"Valerie?"

"He has her."

*Redsaw!* His legs nearly gave out under him as the shock lashed through him. "Is she . . ."

"She is alive, but you must go and save her."

"How? How do I stop him? Can't you come with me? Is she going to . . . to . . . ?"

The glow of the messenger's presence lessened and he touched Axiom-man's shoulder. A rush of calm came over him. "You must do this alone, but trust yourself. Do not waiver. You are equipped to rescue her, but you must go quickly. We will speak again when the time is right."

The messenger glowed bright as he removed his hand from Axiom-man's shoulder and in a flash of light he transformed into a lightning bolt that blasted into the computer screen, leaving Axiom-man alone.

Trembling, Axiom-man clenched his fists and stormed toward the door leading to his balcony. The messenger had left one gift before he departed: Valerie's location imprinted in his mind.

———

A red-glowing fist came crashing down the side of Valerie's head, sending her reeling to the side and slamming into the hard wooden floor. The shock from the energy emitting from Redsaw's hand was akin to sticking one's finger in an electrical socket. Her cheek and teeth vibrated and the splitting headache behind her eyes made her want to scream.

But he had warned her to keep her cries to herself and cemented that fact by breaking two of her fingers. One for each word of "be quiet."

He righted her, picking her chair off the floor and slamming it down hard. "Who is he?"

She spat the blood from her mouth. "I don't . . . I don't know."

"Liar!" He struck her again and sent her crashing down to the other side. Her skull hit the floor and she saw stars. Redsaw was clearly holding back . . . but not by much, it appeared.

Once more, he picked up the chair and slammed it down on the ground.

"You can't fool me. I know you two know each other. Surely there must be something between you," he said.

She ground her teeth and rode the next wave of pain ransacking her head and face. Her neck felt like something had been put out of place and a steel bar had replaced flexible vertebrae, making turning her head near impossible.

Despite how much it hurt, she swore to herself she would never give up Gabriel. "You might as well kill me. I'm not going to talk to you any longer."

"Oh really?" he said and kicked the front legs of the chair. They immediately blew out beneath her, sending her tumbling forward onto her knees. "See, I like you in this position, bowing before me."

She spat at his boots.

He grabbed her by the hair and wrenched her head back. His fingers alit with bright red energy and when he brought them close to her face, the tingling heat coming off them started to burn her skin. She squeezed her eyes shut, tears leaking from their corners.

"Last time: who is he!"

She could sense his fingers getting closer.

Soon he'd pierce her sockets, and burn her eyes out.

All she could manage was to slightly shake her head. He pulled her head back so hard something cracked in her neck as something went out of place then back again. The words almost spilled out. She resolved not to say anything further other than the bare whisper of, "I don't know." He wrenched her head back again, torquing her body along with it. The pain was excruciating and locked up her spine. She screamed, raw and hoarse, the fear and panic kicking into overdrive, months of counselling unraveling all at once and every effort to stay calm completely beyond her control.

The red energy from Redsaw's hands lit up so bright beyond her closed eyes that she squeezed them shut even harder to keep out the light and brace herself for the final blow. The red light grew in intensity and she felt her skin begin to burn. The pain forced her to wail, tremble, her heart to pound.

The loud blast of wood splintering sounded simultaneously as the red light was replaced with a purple one before all went dark.

# CHAPTER TWENTY

Axiom-man plowed straight into Redsaw, bodychecking him and sending them both blasting through the back wall of the wooden tool shed.

The two streaked across the wide grassy field behind the house, which was outside of the city. Red energy crackled around Axiom-man and to save himself from Redsaw striking him, he threw the man off him, sending him hurtling through the air. He touched down and followed up with a long energy blast from his eyes, letting Redsaw have it. Far on the other side of the beam, purple light radiated outward and he felt himself having to send the blast out harder as Redsaw began countering its effects with his own energy.

Axiom-man started walking toward him, utilizing every ounce of power and energy the surge had brought him. The closer he got to Redsaw, the better he could see his nemesis doing the same, with red energy pouring from the man's hands and pressing against the blue energy coming from his eyes.

Quickly, Axiom-man took off into the sky, changing his range of attack. The sudden shift kept Redsaw shooting his energy forward, enabling Axiom-man to zap him from over top and then behind as he came flying in from the rear. He slammed into Redsaw from the back and sent the tyrant face first into the ground. The energy from Redsaw's hands ignited the dry grass of the field. Ignoring the approaching heat, Axiom-man shoved Redsaw's face into the ground and delivered several punches to the back of his head, hoping to knock him out. Redsaw bucked and squirmed beneath him and sent him flying off. Axiom-man tumbled backward and landed hard on his tailbone. Redsaw jumped on him and started wailing on him, just a complete unrestrained beating. No technique. No mercy. The shots landed square against Axiom-man's face, his puffy eyes radiating spikes of heat with each punch. The pain made his whole head sing with searing agony.

Gritting his teeth, he fired at Redsaw's hands with his eye beams. Redsaw's hands lit up red after the first shot and his eye beams seemed to ricochet off the man's fingers, though he hoped he was at least doing some damage.

Bringing in his fists from the side, first one then the other, Axiom-man hook punched Redsaw in the shoulders and neck, the blows as hard as he could muster from his lying position. A repeated effort was enough to slow Redsaw's attack. Seeing stars and still on his back, Axiom-man flew backward along the ground, getting some distance.

*Ignore the pain. Ignore the pain.* He hoped this aura somehow helped keep his injuries at bay or helped lessen the chance of any permanent damage.

He glanced back to the country house some couple hundred yards away past the flames steadily growing on the field. He had radioed Jack on his way over so the Special Force Unit, police and the fire department were probably about ten minutes out if they stepped on it.

He scanned the field for Redsaw. The messenger, it seemed, underestimated Redsaw's strength. The man seemed even stronger compared to when he fought him earlier today. With every death, the more powerful he became and Axiom-man wasn't sure if he could beat Redsaw this night.

Glowing fists surfaced against the night sky and Axiom-man flew up and met them head-on.

*Don't think, just fight, if not for yourself, then for Valerie*, he told himself. He grabbed Redsaw by the wrists and, using his own body like a pendulum, came swinging in with both legs, the balls of his feet connecting square with Redsaw's middle. He heard the man gasp as his diaphragm went up into his ribcage. Taking advantage of the man's moment of weakness, Axiom-man pulled against Redsaw's arms, forcefully tugging him in, and delivered a series of elbows to Redsaw's head.

With a growl, Redsaw lashed out and fired in red energy from the side. Axiom-man flew straight up to avoid it and came down on the other side, getting Redsaw in a bear hug from behind. He was amazed at his superior combat skills then attributed them to everything else he'd done since the last time he and Redsaw fought, and considered maybe there was something true to practice making perfect.

Below, sirens blared and flashing red and blue lights lit up the country road.

Axiom-man hoped Valerie was all right, but couldn't see the rickety old tool shed from this high up.

He tried putting Redsaw in a sleeper, but didn't quite know how to do it, thus affording Redsaw the opportunity to deliver a sharp elbow to his ribs. The guy must've had the boniest elbows Axiom-man ever experienced because it felt like a metal spike had just jabbed his ribcage. He kicked Redsaw off him and meant to follow up with an energy blast, but the approaching vehicles below distracted him.

"Valerie," he said quietly. He had warned Jack that a girl was present. He didn't give names, but Valerie looked so hurt for the brief second he saw her that he couldn't help but wonder if the worst had happened. He knew Jack would recognize her right away since he had been involved with Valerie's case when Bleaken held the city in darkness and Valerie's kidnapping had taken place during it. Now here she was again, taken, and this time *because* of Axiom-man.

Despite fighting the urge at first, Axiom-man gave in and flew a safe distance away from Redsaw and pulled the radio from his belt. "Jack, it's me. She's out back in an old tool shed and white house. Can't miss it. Only one out here. Please get there fast. I don't know if she's alive or . . ." His voice cracked and he couldn't finish.

Jack's voice came through the radio. "I'm on my way. Will round the back of the property on arrival."

"Thanks."

"Gunn out."

Fire lit up Axiom-man's legs as Redsaw poured on the heat, snapping his attention back to the fight.

---

*At least Axiom-man showed up*, Redsaw thought.

He had seen Valerie talk to him outside of Owen Tower and remembered she had flown with him that time long ago when he had attacked Axiom-man in the sky and knocked her from his arms. There was something between them and having her on staff at his company made keeping her close all the easier. As Oscar Owen, he had meant to slowly pull from her Axiom-man's secret identity if she knew it, but all that changed after fighting Axiom-man outside the tower. He had forgotten what it was like to trade blows with him, and upon realizing Axiom-man was stronger than before, plans had to change and approaching Valerie directly under the guise of Redsaw was the best way to do it. She was tough, though, and had an iron will, that was clear. He did his best not to beat her to death, but with each blow he delivered, the more he wanted to end her, the power within him beckoning him in that direction. And if he did do it, her death would make him even stronger and thus make eradicating Axiom-man even easier.

Now, high above the ground and away from the city, he had Axiom-man squirming as the man tried to escape the onslaught of red energy from his hands. Axiom-man tried climbing higher in the sky, but Redsaw kept up with him, firing shot after shot of red energy at Axiom-man's legs and body. The man twitched and spun with each blow.

The two ascended higher, the burning field below getting smaller and smaller, the lights of the city blurring more and more off in the distance.

Redsaw gave it everything he had, ignoring the chill on the air the higher they went.

———

Each blast from Redsaw's hands was excruciating and Axiom-man wouldn't be surprised if later, when he peeled off his uniform, he'd find burn marks all over his legs.

If he survived this.

*Going to have to do something about armor,* he thought as he grimaced with each zap of energy against him. Between the bullet wound to his leg and now this endless onslaught of Redsaw's energy beams, he wondered if he'd even walk again if he survived the night.

He fired off energy beams of his own. Redsaw took a few head on and dodged others.

Swallowing the pain, Axiom-man kept reaching toward the heavens. Soon, this would all be over.

---

Redsaw's head began to spin and he couldn't figure out why. Was it all this exertion after so much time away? Axiom-man picked up speed above him. Redsaw kicked it into high gear himself. The ground was so far below that the fire in the field was as small as a penny.

Coughing, Redsaw tried to get air into his lungs but found none was coming. He kept coughing the higher they went until even that ceased and each reflex to inhale was met with zero oxygen.

Then he understood. *Clever.* He let himself begin to fall, still firing off rounds of red energy. Axiom-man was still going up and getting so far away it was difficult to see him. Very quickly, Axiom-man disappeared against the night sky altogether.

No matter. At least Redsaw was starting to breathe again.

What felt like a freight train plowed into him from behind and grabbed hold of him, taking him back up into the sky.

"No!" he shouted and wrestled against Axiom-man's grip on him. He thrashed his head back, headbutting Axiom-man in what he hoped was the nose. He heard the man grunt.

They still went higher and he couldn't breathe again. Axiom-man increased his hold, going into a full-fledged bear hug. Quickly, darkness started to rim Redsaw's vision and buzzing filled his ears.

*No!* He grabbed hold of Axiom-man's forearms and poured as much energy from his hands into them as he could.

Axiom-man yelled and let go.

Redsaw dove downward and flew as fast as he could to lower airspace.

A blast of blue energy zapped past him. Did Axiom-man streak by? How did he move so fast?

Another blast on his right. What?

He wasn't thinking straight. He was being shot at. It wasn't Axiom-man flying by then doubling back then flying by then—

The neckline of his cape lurched against his throat in a sudden jolt, the pressure on his windpipe making it feel like he swallowed a stone. He flew against the pull of his cape against his neck. The pressure from going in the opposite direction was soon unbearable and he had to stop. With a violent twist, he was hurled high into the sky. He somersaulted backward through the air, higher and higher. Axiom-man flew into him and took him up and up.

His lungs ached like all get out and buzzing filled his ears again. Soon, the darkness rimming his vision returned. He beat against Axiom-man's body. The man took it—grunting—but took it.

Head spinning, he wasn't sure what was going on anymore and he felt his awareness slipping further and further away.

He wanted to say no or stop or let go . . . but he couldn't get his lips to move.

White light filled his vision and for a brief second he saw they were passing through the Earth's atmosphere, the awe-inspiring sight of the curvature of the Earth glowing against the blackness of space.

Then darkness.

Silence.

Nothing.

# CHAPTER TWENTY-ONE

REDSAW'S BODY WENT limp in Axiom-man's arms. He rose even higher just to deprive him of oxygen a little longer before needing to take him back down and making sure his breathing started up again.

Somewhere below, Valerie was hurt. He'd have to go lower so the radio unit would be in range and he could check in with Jack.

*Oh Valerie, I'm sorry. Oh so sorry.* Tears glazed his eyes. *He found you. It wouldn't have happened if not for me.* He blinked away the tears. *What have I done?*

As he descended, he wondered if he should just kill Redsaw right now. It would put an end to everything that was supposed to happen and pay him back for what he had done to Valerie.

Axiom-man recently swore he would never kill anyone after that incident with the werewolves, but was there an exception here with Redsaw? Would stopping one man in the interest of saving the lives of many be an excuse to murder? Was it murder or a pre-emptive strike? Were they or could they be the same thing? Would it be justice for the lives he stole? For Valerie?

He wasn't sure. His mind said yes, but his heart said otherwise. As he descended, he listened carefully for Redsaw's breathing to resume. It finally did at around ten thousand feet.

With Redsaw unconscious in his arms, this was prime opportunity to find out who the man really was. He eyed Redsaw's mask and assumed it would simply pull back like a hood. With Redsaw's back to him, he'd have to flip him around to see his face after removing it. He reached over and slid his fingers into the tops of the eye holes in the mask and pulled it backward. The man had black hair, blowing in the high altitude wind.

Redsaw twitched.

*Hurry.* "Let's see who you are," he said. His mind flashed to Valerie and he wondered if she was okay. *I should've made him pay.* Anger swelled within and he decided to end it now and consequences be damned. He couldn't fulfill his promise not to kill. Not like this. Not with him. "I want to see the face of the murderer before he dies."

"Not today." Redsaw jerked and grabbed hold of Axiom-man's arms with red, glowing hands. The burst of pain made Axiom-man let go and Redsaw kicked off him, sending him tumbling against the night sky. A blast of red energy struck him in the chest, keeping him spinning backward.

When he finally righted himself, Redsaw was gone.

*I was so close!* He'd hesitated. Should he have done what needed doing and just . . . killed him instead of debating it? He gathered his breath and waited for his racing heart to slow. Deliberating had been the right choice.

But he had considered killing.

He could only imagine how disappointed the messenger must be in him if he was watching.

Axiom-man scanned the surrounding sky and even looked down to the ground below. The fire in the field seemed to have been put out. He couldn't see the flashing sirens by the country house but he could've been too high in the air for that.

There was no sign of Redsaw.

Hurting all over, he leaned forward, put his hands out, and flew downward.

The radio on his belt came to life with Jack's voice. "You there? This is at least the fourth time I've tried to get you on this thing. So you know, we got her. She's fine. Well, not fine, but she's alive."

Axiom-man took the radio off his belt and said, "Copy that. Thank you. I'll be there in a moment."

*Valerie.* Thinking of her and wanting revenge for what Redsaw did had distracted him and potentially cost him—perhaps even the world—everything.

––––––––––

Still spacey, Redsaw flew as fast as he could away from the field, Axiom-man, all of it. He had his mask back in place and headed straight for Owen Tower. Once he arrived, he landed on the balcony to the penthouse suite, entered the security code on the panel by the double sliding glass door, and went in.

He pulled his mask off, relieved Axiom-man hadn't seen his face. Had he been just some guy, he wouldn't have been recognized anyway, but Oscar Owen was well known these days and surely Axiom-man would've known who he was. At least with his identity still a secret, he could come and go as he pleased, be Redsaw as he pleased, and not have to worry about outside interference as long as he wasn't tracked back here or to his home just outside the city.

In an instant, it had all finally caught up with him. The masquerade, the deaths, the power . . . . He hadn't meant for it to snowball like it had. He simply wanted Axiom-man removed, but he knew that wasn't possible now. The dark power within him was too strong and made him kill without regret. Even now . . . he was fine with it because it served a greater purpose. It was time to embrace what he'd become and wearing the Redsaw suit again enabled him to do that, to let go and indulge in the power within. It was time to finally see how powerful he could be as long as he didn't hold back.

A figure made of shadow materialized out of the dark, its humanoid form only visible thanks to the little bit of moonlight coming in through the window.

Oscar immediately pulled his mask back into place.

"No need to hide yourself," the figure said. Its voice was male, raspy.

He sent off a blast of red energy straight at the shadow man. It passed through him and blew a hole in the wall beyond.

"Don't bother," the being said.

"What do you want?"

"I have a message for you."

---

Axiom-man stood at Valerie's side, holding her hand. She was on a gurney and about to go into an ambulance. She had an oxygen mask over her face and her eyes and cheeks were swollen, bathed in black and blue.

"I'm sorry," he said.

She simply looked at him and he wasn't sure if she could hear him.

To the paramedic, he asked, "Is she going to be okay?"

"She received major trauma to the head and has a severe concussion. She's conscious, but her state of awareness isn't quite there. She should come around in the next few hours. Now, please, we need to take her. The longer we delay . . ."

He nodded and leaned in close to her and whispered, "I'm sorry. I'll be by to see you soon."

He let go of her hand, sick to his stomach that she had gotten hurt again. He had thought that maybe, just maybe, things would turn out for the better for both of them. With her finding out who he was and the newfound freedom from absence of secrets, he thought that was possible. But she was a target and Redsaw clearly handpicked her.

She wasn't safe anymore as long as that tyrant was still out there.

The city wasn't safe anymore either.

And he had let Redsaw get away.

# CHAPTER TWENTY-TWO

GABRIEL SAT ON the hospital bed while Valerie was in the room's bathroom getting dressed. She'd been in St. Boniface Hospital all week. So had he. Not only was he keeping guard, he spent the last seven days profusely apologizing and a week of "I'm sorrys" seemed to be Valerie's limit because last night she finally told him to shut up. She said she understood the risk and cost of knowing him. Just didn't expect it to happen so soon.

She had asked why he wasn't at work, and instead of saying he was on vacation, he came clean and told her: "Rob fired me."

"I'm so sorry," she replied. "Why?"

"Attendance. One too many times Axiom-man got in the way. To be fair, he cut me a lot of slack, but the time came, I guess."

"That sucks. Will you be okay?"

"I'm fine."

"I meant, are you able to take care of yourself?"

He relayed his short term plan and some of the money coming in, but confessed he wasn't sure what was going to happen since he didn't have a new job yet.

"If things get bad, you can room with me."

"Sleepovers?" It was a stupid question, but it just kind of came out.

"You could say that."

Gabriel stood, stretched, and looked himself over in the mirror. He looked like he'd been hit by a truck. He purposely didn't sleep much this week so he could keep an eye on Valerie. The injuries to his face made it look like an old catcher's mitt. The swelling had gone down but things were misshapen. When the doctors and nurses who came in and out of the room saw him, they immediately identified what happened and told him he'd have to arrange for surgery and, most likely, a couple of them. He thanked them for their advice, but stuck to the T3s and ice packs for now. He was embarrassed by his appearance, however, and wondered how Valerie could even look at him.

Not that she fared any better. The swelling was gone, but the bruising remained, painting her beautiful face in a mosaic of yellow and purple blotches. Her broken fingers were in splints and every bit of her exposed skin was spotted with bruises, too.

After being discharged, they took a cab to her place. The cabbie gave them a curious glance because of how they looked, but kept his questions to himself.

He entered her suite first.

He had called the super while she was in hospital and explained there was a break-in. A new balcony window was already in place. Valerie walked around the room, presumably to check everything was as she left it.

"Can I get you anything?" he asked.

Her eyes bore a heavy sadness. "Just wondering if it's even safe here. Somehow he knew my name, was able to find out where I lived. He must've seen us together. He said he knew we knew each other."

"I'm so sorry," Gabriel said. "I don't know how that happened. I thought I had kept you out of it, kept things separate." *Unless he recognized her from that time we flew together, but that was so long ago.*

"He might've seen us at the opening."

"But I barely talked to you." She started to sniffle then burst into an all-out cry. Pain for her flooded his heart as he came and put his arms around her. He kissed the side of her head and held her close while she shook in his arms.

———

Plans were underway for three Owen Towers to be built across the country, one in Toronto, another in Vancouver and yet another in Montreal. If Oscar had his way, a handful of other cities would follow soon.

He had called Valerie several times over the past week to see "where she was," even went so far as threatening her job if she didn't return to work. Ultimately, he knew he'd never go through with it, not with her possibly knowing who Axiom-man was.

He had tried the hospitals but admittance refused to give out any information. He'd try her again in a few days, and he was certain there was no way she knew who he really was and was purposefully avoiding him. The Special Force Unit, even Axiom-man, would've already made their move if that was the case.

So far as the city was concerned, the storm had abruptly stopped and Redsaw had once again disappeared. Which wasn't true. After daylight, he kept to the shadows, and picked off people one by one: some locally, some in another city, some in yet another city, making each look like a random murder, nothing spectacular.

At least, not yet.

# EPILOGUE

THAT EVENING, AXIOM-MAN held Valerie in his arms as he took her into the air. She held onto him tight and smiled the whole time, her grin outshining the bruises on her face.

"It's so beautiful up here," she said.

"You can see everything."

"How's your face? Your leg? Your hand?"

"I've been worse for wear, but they hurt. I'm going to have to see somebody. Just don't know how I'm going to explain away the injuries other than I got royally beat up by a gang and was too scared to tell anyone, but ended up coming forward because the pain was too much. I don't know. I deserve it for what I let happen to you."

"Gabriel, stop it."

"I do, Val. You nearly died *again* because I wasn't there to protect you."

"It's not your job, not in the way you think it is."

"How can you say that?"

"I never want to be a burden to you, and I never want you to put me or my safety above anyone else's. You need to treat me the same as everyone else that way. Axiom-man can't play favorites."

"But he does. But *I* do. I love you, Valerie, with everything I've got."

"I love you, too, and because I do, I won't let Axiom-man not be all he can be because of me."

Those were the three words he had yearned to hear for the longest time, and they melted his heart. He just hoped there would be a future where they could exchange those words freely, without restraint, always with hope and promise.

He remembered the messenger's words about dark days coming if he didn't stop Redsaw. Now with Redsaw gone and seemingly in hiding again, he wondered exactly how those dark days would come about and if he should tell her about it. "I'm going to need your help with that. My mission isn't over. I don't think it will be until Redsaw's put away for good."

She seemed to absorb his words and was silent a few moments before saying, "I'll help you in any way I can, and I'll start by saying you need to do something about your costume."

"I know. Tights aren't cutting it anymore."

"Why did you pick tights to begin with?"

"Main reason was so I can take my suit anywhere and any kind of armor wouldn't work beneath regular clothes."

"Well, you need something else. You can't keep getting shot at and getting your face rearranged every time you go up against someone as strong as you."

"I'm not sure how much a helmet would help against a guy like Redsaw."

"At least consider a bulletproof vest."

"You know how expensive those are? I don't even have a job."

"I'll pay for it. I called into work earlier and said I'd be back next week. Thought he was going to fire me, especially after that last message he left. He sounded so angry."

"Well, you did kind of fall off the grid for a week and after a major disaster at the company to boot."

"True."

They flew in silence for a few moments and he couldn't help himself but bring it up one more time.

"I know I keep saying it, but I'm so sorry you got hurt. It's my fault and, I don't know how to say this, but if you want to go slower or call it quits, I'll totally understand."

"Just stop."

"Sorry."

"No, I mean *stop*."

"Oh." He slowed down and eventually paused mid-air, righted them, and hovered.

She slowly peeled down his mask. "I'm not going to quit on you. In that shed, I thought about it, what the possibility would look like. When he wanted to know your real name—he didn't know for sure that I knew it—I thought for all of a quarter second about saying it. And in that quarter second, when I imagined doing it, my heart broke at betraying you. I'm in this for the long haul, Gabriel, and I'd rather die than give up on you and on us." She grabbed his face and pressed her lips hard against his, then she eased the pressure and kissed him passionately.

He closed his eyes and returned the kiss in kind. When she pulled away, she smiled and said, "Think maybe we can go a little faster?"

With a smile, he pulled his mask into place and then leaned forward. "Hang on."

As he started to pick up speed, she said, "I wasn't talking about the flight."

# About the Author

**A.P. Fuchs** is the author of many novels and short stories. His most recent books are *Axiom-man: Outlaw; Axiom-man: Episode No. 2: Underground Crusade; Getting Down and Digital: How to Self-publish Your Book; Look, Up on the Screen! The Big Book of Superhero Movie Reviews; Canadian Scribbler: Collected Letters of an Underground Writer;* and *Redemption of the Dead*, the third book in his time travel zombie trilogy.

Also a cartoonist, he is known for his superhero series, *The Axiom-man Saga*, both in novel and comic book format. Please see **www.axiom-man.com** for more on this series.

Fuchs's main website is **www.canisterx.com**

# THE
# AXIOM-MAN™
## SAGA

AN ONGOING SUPERHERO BOOK SERIES
BY A.P. FUCHS

Available in paperback and eBook
at your favorite online retailer like Amazon.com

# WHAT HAPPENS WHEN METAHUMANS FACE OFF AGAINST THE DEADLIEST FOES?

## WELCOME TO THE EXCITING WORLD OF

## AN ONGOING SUPERHERO ANTHOLOGY SERIES
### EDITED BY A.P. FUCHS

Available in paperback and eBook
at your favorite online retailer like Amazon.com